COVER ART BY LISA VASQUEZ

ISBN-13: 978-1461031086
ISBN-10: 1461031087

THE UNSAINTLY

By Lisa Vasquez

Condemn me to my belly; I'll still walk all over you.

Dear Joe —
thank you for
being an inspiration
to me

FROM THE AUTHOR, A WORD.

If you're reading this book, now, it means that I have finally finished writing down the beginning of Isabel's story. In doing so, I feel compelled to tell you a few things, first.

When I began this book, I had no idea that it would become what it has. It took a life of its own and poured from my heart as a symbol of the strife and pursuit of my soul to look upon the face of God and to find my own salvation.

There are things you will read in this book that are disturbing and while I make no apologies for that – it is after all, Isabel's journey – I will have compassion for those that have more delicate sensibilities. Consider this your warning. It is not a build-up. It is not to a way to set up this book to be "more than it delivers". Take it as you will and know that as its author, it was as hard to write it. It was one thing to see the scenes in my head, but another thing to share them. It left me vulnerable. I weighed back and forth whether I should even let another person read them.

Then I said, "To Hell with it."

In closing – I believe in a higher power. I believe in Evil. I believe that we are all connected to one another in spirit, regardless of race, religion, and all the other bullshit. Turn us inside out and we are all same color. I dared to write this book. Do you dare to read it?

I hope that it questions your faith and your beliefs. Because if your faith is never questioned, you will never *truly* believe.

WITHOUT **DARKNESS** THERE CAN BE NO **LIGHT**

PROLOGUE

It was a warm, clear summer sky over the trail to the private garden of one of the monasteries in the south of France. During the hour following lunch and prayers, many of the clergy would tend to the garden.

Among the meticulously cared for roses were statues so lifelike it felt as though they would turn and move at any moment. Saints with upturned eyes gazing infinitely into heaven were accompanied by angels with open wings playing with doves in the small ponds that trickled with the sounds of the fountain centered in it. Rows and rows of flowers teased the senses. The aroma was not one that could easily be forgotten as each breeze brought about another waft of fragrance released from the petals that waved gently on the air.

Two men in particular, dressed in monks' robes, followed the cobble stoned path to a more private area where benches would give them a place to sit. The soft rustling of their hems passed over their sandals and they both held their hands clasped within large brown sleeves. The man on the left kept his oversized cowl low over his face, shadowing his features while the other had his hood down, soaking in the light of the day.

Finding a secluded table, the older one was pleased to see the ornate table was topped with marble chess pieces carved by the hands of the monks inside. He motioned to the empty seat across from him and the other chuckled before accepting the offer, sitting down.

The duo seemed deeply engaged in quiet conversation, leaning in as they took turns responding. Every so often one would look over their shoulder or around to keep their eye on their surroundings. Sometimes, one would even laugh and shake his head at a comment made by the other.

Every now and then, between conversations a piece was moved by one and the other would quietly contemplate his counter. As light as the topic may have appeared to be, the tension of competition radiated out from both of them.

"This is an age old debate between us" the man on the left said. He then peered up from under his hood at the old man on his right side. His companion smiled and looked up at the heavens, crystal blue eyes rivaled any ocean and his hair was a brilliant white, betraying his age and wisdom.

The clergy around them never seemed to take much notice of them as they sat there. The older male on the right removed his purse and opened it to stick his hand inside and throw out some stale crumbs for the birds that appeared to be drawn to him. Some would sit on his shoulder and sing beautiful songs that birds were never heard to sing. He smiled at his new feathered friends then leaned forward sliding his piece over a few squares (Nb1-c3, Bc8-g4)[1].

"So it is. But do I not know all things?" was the reply.

"That has never been proven" Grinned the dark man, sliding another piece into place.

"Hasn't it?" replied the white haired gentleman.

A frown came over the older man's opponent at the move and he refocused on the board as he responded. Agitation was starting to show through in his voice as he lifted his piece and slid it into position (h2-h3, Bg4xf3).

"You always make it seem as if you knew I would question you. I disagree. I think you were shocked to find out that free will was

---

[1] (Chernev, 2012)

a natural progression of my creation. I was your first, after all." He chided. "The one made most like your image."

"You're a spoiled child, Lucifer. You always have been."

"Ah, but father, you made me this way and then you cast me away? Discarded like rubbish?" The dark man hissed his reply. "That will make this event all the more, sweeter. I shall, once more, taint your current fascination. I will once again be that thorn in your side. I will *never* let you know peace."

Though his expression did not change, the older man's face grew stern. It was a subtle shift in the air temperature which started to drop and announce the impending storm. The familiar chill to the air carried on it, the smell of the ocean to mix with the garden's perfume and the power of the storm began to build strength pulling the nimbus clouds into a swarm like agitated bees.

"You can shut the door, Father, but I will not be ignored" Lucifer condemned.

Then the man with the shadowed features stood up, bowing his head. Even after their tense conversation and harsh words he showed reverence, however resentful it was. No response was shown to the one who still had his head lowered, by the elder; the man seemed to be instead, struggling to control an underlying wrath.

Slowly lifting his head, glowing eyes from under the large cowl met the rigid face of his father. Lucifer growled then turned on his heel, stalking off into the distance.

EXODUS - LUCIFER

His head and his hairs were *white like wool, as white as snow; and his eyes were as a flame of fire*

- *Revelation 1:14*

AND I SHALL GIVE THEM THE MORNING STAR…

The heavens rumbled with thunder. Skies that went on forever in cerulean, bled with hues of deep crimson and amber. There was a war going on: Father versus Son in the quest for independence, dominance and escape from rule. Dressed in brilliant white robes, an overlay of gold and chromium, the Father stood seething with pure wrath awaiting the approach of the prisoner. When they entered the chambers lined by pillars and the praetorian legion of soldier angels, the King of Heaven pivoted and closed the steps to greet them.

"Lucifer, what have you done!" He shouted, his hand whipping across the perfect visage of his creation's face, marring the reflection that mirrored his own.

Lucifer's head fell to the side at the blow and he spit out the thick, black blood that filled his mouth before responding, "Taken what is rightfully ours!"

"Rightfully?" God laughed. "I *created* you – and I can unmake you just as swiftly." God was leaning in, now. His eyes filled with lightning and swarming clouds, grey like the storm.

The Praetorian Guard broke their stillness, each one turning to look upon the other. From behind them, the ranks began to fill the chambers as the chaos continued around them. Lucifer had conducted the mutiny and uprising of his brothers and sisters who were now slaughtering one another just beyond the protection of this room.

Lucifer turned his gaze upward to meet his Creator's eyes. Mirrored irises reflected the madness that his maker bore down on him, now, even as he struggled against the chains that bound him. The guards on either side remained unmoving but he could sense the uneasiness within them. Lucifer was the first. The strongest. The most dangerous of all of them. He was their trainer, and their master, second only to Lord God himself.

Lucifer was about to lunge forward when the doors burst open and another ran toward them and collapsed to his knees between the two poised males.

"Father, please!" The newly arrived angel turned and looked between them, pleadingly before pressing his face to the marble floor at God's feet. "My father is touched with madness, Holy Lord. He knows not what he does. Spare him…Please, spare him!"

Lucifer's eyes filled with fear for a moment. His son, Raphael was pleading for his life which meant that he would give up his own. "Raphael, no!"

Fighting now with all his might against the chains, God's face tightened and contorted with the pain of the decision. Lucifer was his most loved and prized creation. Raphael was his son, born with the heart of bravery, compassion and love for mankind.

"Do you see, Lucifer?" His voice cracked with the breaking of his heart as he spoke to the angel being restrained before him. "This is why I created you. *Compassion*, and duty."

Lucifer's face was wrought with torment and disdain for his Maker, his wings bound behind him were fighting to be free but the weights and shackles were heavy, forcing him into the position he was in. It infuriated him even more.

"Compassion." He spit the words out like a poison he could not stand to taste upon his tongue. "Compassion for the mortals that defy you?! Who turn their backs on you! They are pitiful and weak at heart and soul. WE give you our will, our love, and our loyalty and you chain us to protecting the filth you have spread out across the earth!"

Lucifer's words ended with him lunging forward, only to be jerked back by the two guards beside him.

Raphael crawled to his father and continued to beg for him be still, "Father, please! Why are you doing this?"

Lucifer's heart raced with conflict. The brilliance of the beating muscle shone through the translucent skin of his chest, before dimming slightly again, "My son…" Tears fell from his eyes then, remembering his mother who was now banished from Heaven for the shame of their transgression. The mortals were paired, could mate and create children but angels were forbidden this kind of freedom. They were merely the employers of God's law. They were merely his soldiers, watchers, and entertainment. He spoke, they acted. Because of God's affection for his first "born" creation, he spared Raphael in hopes that it would bring

Lucifer back to the bosom of the King, but instead it made Lucifer's plight that much stronger.

Without warning, Lucifer's wings shattered the weights and chains, his form rose to its full height, and his heart illuminated brightly with such force that the guards at his side had to shield their eyes, "I do this for you!"

Suddenly, with sword drawn, Lucifer ran at God unleashing a scream. The pillars shook around them until they began to weaken and fall upon the ranks beneath them. Seeing the intent of their former General, the soldiers were called to attention prompting action with intent on stopping the attack on the King. Just as Lucifer had reached the steps and thrust out his sword, the world around him slowed to a crawl and the sound of a horn filled the air stunning him with the decibel of its power and vibration. Every single piece of matter around him was completely still, from the falling debris to the swarm of soldiers. Though he could not move he was aware when God's voice filled his mind.

"For your crimes, you shall be imprisoned beneath the bowels of the earth. To crawl under those you hold such contempt for until such time as you learn humility, and love." God's voice broke again and Lucifer watched as his Creator's hand twisted his sword so that the edge glinted with power. The sound of the blade cutting through the air was a sound that Lucifer would never forget, for all eternity.

Noooo! He screamed within his mind and witnessed the execution of his son, Raphael. A sacrifice made by God to save Lucifer's soul.

The world came into focus again. Debris exploded around him like shrapnel and the guards were thrown away. Raphael's body fell limply in slow motion to the floor as Lucifer ran to catch him. The blood of his only son poured like wine over his fingers even as Lucifer tried to press his palms to the wound in effort to make it stop. Raphael tried to speak but the gash in his throat made it impossible. He choked and gurgled fearfully, then fell quiet.

"Shh, my son." The words could barely be choked from his Father's mouth. He felt the life of his child slipping and his energy, the life source that he was made of, snaking up through his own arms, until he was completely absorbed. Raphael's physical body slowly dispersed into light and then faded like a star in the distant universe.

The room around him continued to tremble and the world continued to be showered in blood rain. Lucifer did not care. A world away, he heard the scream of Raphael's mother raise up and fill the skies like a dragon's cry. Holding his head in his hands, he continued to kneel among the chaos to mourn his son before finally the madness consumed him whole.

"It is time for you to go, Lucifer. I can no longer look upon thee." God turned his face from Lucifer and began to walk away. The guards had surrounded the King, protectively, as they moved in silent footsteps to the entrance of the tower.

With a hiss, Lucifer stood up again and extended his razor tipped wings in all their glory, aiming his sword at his Creator, "Condemn me to my belly; I'll *still* walk all over you." Lucifer had raised his own army and they began to close in.

Turning to the sound of gathering masses, God's eyes widened. He looked upon his ranks of angels who had collaborated with their brother and betrayed their King. They had witnessed the slaying of Raphael, and now they were there to claim blood for blood.

In a last minute decision to end all the bloodshed, and to save the lives of the angels that remained in his service, God released the final command which ended Lucifer's ability to enter Heaven, ever again. The floors opened up and universe cracked, sending darkness swirling in. The whirlwind was more than even Lucifer could fend off. The black hole roared and inhaled, stretching further and further around them until each angel who stood at his side was dragged down into the abyss.

Lucifer, who wanted only unchained will and freedom to love, became consumed by his hate and anger. He climbed atop his own throne and ruled over the Fallen with an unforgiving hand. They had no choice but to follow him and do his bidding with the ultimate goal of destroying everything that God held dear.

REVELATOR - ISABEL

The year is 1254. Having exhausted all his funds and a dire need for him to be home with this family, Louis IX of France returns home. Pope Innocent IV excommunicates Rudolph I of Germany who would later become the Holy Roman Emperor. By the end of the year, Pope Alexander IV succeeds Pope Innocent IV.

She was breathing. The painful expanding and contracting of her of her ribcage told her that and the only sound that she could hear was the sound of her own breathing in the still of the darkness that surrounded her. A darkness that was so thick that even with her eyes open she could see nothing. Her body ached like she'd been beaten for days and she could feel her skin, cold as a corpse, wrapped around her body to try and stop shivering.

It brought back childhood memories of a time when Louis and she played hide and seek. Isabel hid in mother's closet one afternoon but got locked in. At first she thought it was fun. She played in all mother's dresses until the minutes which seemed like hours ticked away until she realized, suddenly, she could not hear anything outside the door. What a great hiding spot! Louis would never find her here. Isabel sat down on the floor and began to crawl under the hems of gowns, letting the material brush over her face. The small sliver of light from under the door just off in the distance when she saw a shadow run past, causing her to freeze where she was. She had to remain silent or Louis would find her, and win. Rolling back to sit on her heels, Isabel leaned further into the darkness and felt the prickling of danger, raising the hairs on the back of her neck. Something was there with her.

She remembered, now, screaming and banging on the large oak door. The sound of the brass handle jiggling was still fresh in her mind. Another blood curdling scream and the light finally washed in, blinding her momentarily as the nanny opened the door and reached for her, snatching her small arm to jerk her to safety. The sound of Louis' laughter could be heard and Isabel cradled the crook of her arm over her eyes to shield them from the offending light. She remembered the feeling of how heavy the thumping of her heart in her small chest was while being chastised by the woman, and ridiculed by her sibling.

Isabel curled into a fetal position letting the memory fade away. She tried to cry but there was no moisture in her mouth or her eyes. She could only weep in dry silence. Her entire small frame shook with despair.

Just like the closet door letting in the light when she was seven, the light rushed in and blinded her, now. This light was different. This light was brighter. It was pure like sunlight. She lifted her hand upward to protect her vision which had grown used to the darkness. Sensitive eyes squinted at the offensive brightness and tried to focus on her surroundings.

All Isabel could see was the blood that dripped from her hands and along her arms. Smeared trails of blood and dirt made their winding path to her torn and ragged fingertips. Crying out, she gasped and wrung her hands together to try and clean them. She was crying again. The realization of what happened flooded her, pulling her into their smothering depths.

"No!" she screamed.

She was grabbing her skirts now trying to spit on the material to rub off the blood. Looking down, she saw that it was everywhere. It was futile to try and clean it but she could not stop herself. Panic swept in and she began screaming louder, rocking her body and repeating the word over and over again. *No! No! No!*

"Nooo!!" there was no echo and the sound assaulted her own ears.

The morning light had trickled into the room along with the cool draft of winter's air, taking with it the nightmare that continued to claim her, repeatedly, for the past few months. Isabel stirred in her sleep, curling up deeper into her thick, wool blanket. Shivering a little, she'd squint and bring her knees up so that she was in the fetal position, again. Just as she was about to fall back asleep when she was awakened to the chill once more moving against her feet. Using her toes to tug the blanket down, she avoided full consciousness for another five minute's rest. Beginning to shiver, yet again, pulled her out of the sleep world. Opening one eye, she gazed down to see the blankets were off her legs. She sighed and tugged them over her body, cocooning into it but the blankets were suddenly jerked off of her and thrown into a crumpled heap at the bottom of the bed.

With a gasp, she sat up and looked around, expecting to see someone there; another nun, Father Raphael or anyone. Even with the first light of morning, the grey was too dark to see much of anything so Isabel scooted to the top of her meager bed, drawing her knees to her chest. Tucking her freezing toes within the hem of her nightgown, she wrapped her arms around herself. Her hand began to tremor slightly and she grasped it with the other to still it, paying no mind to it, other than fear and cold.

"Just dreams," she'd say aloud to herself.

Standing up from her bed, Isabel lit the candle beside her and shuffled into her shoes. She walked to the window to gaze outside and saw Marciel walking in the garden. A man she'd never seen before was at his side. The two seemed engrossed in conversation and Isabel wondered if he was just a visitor or if he was new to their town. She smiled a bit then backed up, closing the shutter to her window so that she could begin her morning prayers and dress for the day.

Setting the candle on the small table, she kneeled in front of the crucifix on her wall and made the sign of the cross. When she bowed her head, she could feel a sour churning of her bowels before nausea rose up in her throat. It was so sudden that Isabel was drawn forward to one hand and felt as if the temperature in the room rose twenty degrees, enveloping her in a wave of heat. Confusion set in and she braced herself just as the pain welled up inside her once more.

"Oh God," she whispered but the rest of the sentence was cut off.

She felt the familiar rush of saliva to her lips which had grown dry and the trembling of her lower jaw that preceded the inevitable; her body was forced forward again and she suddenly felt choked. The scraping in her throat brought about a new pain, even more severe, and she tried with all her might to help it up. Something was lodged in her throat.

She gasped in small doses as often as she could but whatever was in there was tearing its way out and scraping against the tender flesh of her esophagus. Tears swelled in her eyes and she rocked back and forth, afraid she would die from lack of oxygen. Another dry heave and she could feel it on the back of her tongue now. She was disoriented. She had to be. It felt like something metal. *Metal!? What is going on?!* Reaching an unsteady, fumbling hand up, she dug her fingers into her mouth and scratched desperately to pull whatever it was, out. Her fingertips found the edge, which was sharp and thick. Finally getting a grasp on it, she tugged but the end seemed lodged in the small, enclosed walls of her throat. Her gasps turned to small wheezes and Isabel could feel the tingling of dark spots that came when one was about to lose consciousness.

More desperate now, she pulled without care of the damage that was being dealt to her throat. Saliva mixed with blood fell in long thick strands from her lower lip, the fingers of the hand that held her weight curled against the floor. *I can't breathe!* She screamed inside her mind. The object was growing slippery but she continued to pull until finally it moved. She pulled the object from between her lips and a trail of something long followed, seeming to come up from her belly. Shaky fingers slid over what looked like small stones, but her vision was still blurred and the threat of unconsciousness still lingered on the outer edges of her tunneling vision.

Finally! She was able to dislodge the foreign object before passing out, dropping it she heard it clatter to the floor amid the spit and blood. Isabel rushed to her feet still lightheaded, nearly falling as she reached out for the candle and then collapsed to her knees again. She lowered the candle to the floor, lowering her face to inspect the area. What she saw ripped through her with a fear so deep, she feared for her very soul. Setting the candle down, she fought back the coughing sensation caused from the itchy, scrapes against her tonsils. There was no denying what it was that was in her throat. Sliding her fingers through the blood and spit, she grasped it not believing it was real. It was her rosary!

Isabel's teary eyes fixated on it for a long moment, lacking understanding. How could this be lodged in her throat? Had she gone mad? The sounds of the bells outside sent her reeling and she nearly knocked the candle over. Afraid of what was happening; Isabel quickly hid the rosary under the make-shift mattress of her bed and cleaned up the mess of fluid off the floor. Pushing it to the back of her mind, she did her best to look presentable. She threw her clothing on and ran out to meet the others for morning prayers, Lauds, chores, and breakfast.

Descent From Grace - Marciel

When Isabel passed me that morning as I was coming in from the garden, she looked pale and worried. I felt something in her that I had never felt since knowing her. She was normally tranquil and full of peace but now she looked as though she was running scared. The other nuns bustled around her quietly and quickly but Isabel seemed lost. I watched her look over her shoulder several times before being nudged by Miriam toward their destination, and Isabel nearly dropped her bible. She caught it just before it landed on the stones before I noticed that her hand was trembling.

I nodded a hello to her as she brushed past me with her head down and caught a glimpse of blood against her collar. I frowned, concerned for her well-being but turned back to the way I was walking then paused when something caught my attention. Something was on the ground where she had almost dropped her bible. I moved toward it and realized it was Isabel's rosary. Picking it up, I quickly rushed back out to return it to her. It took me a couple of light jogs but I finally caught up with her and placed my hand on her elbow, "Isabel, you dropped this."

She tried to smile but I could see it was not genuine. Her trembling hand turned upward to receive the rosary and I cupped mine underneath, spilling the beads into her palm. Almost at once, she began a violent coughing fit. The other nuns shot me a glare drenched in angry silence then rushed toward their holy sister to assist her. I felt *the sickness* in her but I did not want to believe it. Stepping back, I kept my gaze on her, consumed by worry.

From behind, Father Dulante spoke, "Is she alright?"

"Yes," I said a little too hastily, and then smiled a bit to cover the truth of my concern. "She is fine. She probably just caught a chill."

Father Dulante tugged his robes to his body a little more, nodding agreeably, "Yes, it is unseasonably cold."

His breath hung on the air between us.

"We should get inside before we catch it, too. Father Raphael doesn't allow for us to take ill. The Lord's work does not sleep, right?"

I grinned at him and he laughed.

"Careful, Marciel, I think he has ears on every flower" he said. He reached out to pat my arm and started to walk toward the chapel when his words seemed to cause the hair to stand up on my arms.

"Come! Let us go to morning prayers, brother!"

As much as I tried to stay focused, I could not. After morning prayers I brought the soiled laundry to the lay women to be cleaned but knocked over a bucket of water. I was thoroughly chastised for my clumsiness before being shoo'ed back out. Being mortal was hard. As much empathy as we Angels had toward humans, and as much jealousy as some of us could muster, I could never conceive how easy it was to be what WE were.

I guess at this point it would make sense for me to introduce myself. My given name is Marciel. As often is the case, I was sent by God to watch and record the life of one mortal. In this case, it was Isabel. Posing as human, I took a humble position in the sanctum. I would clean up after the elderly who were afflicted with leprosy. I would clean their bandages, change their bedding and sit with them. Sometimes, they just needed to have someone listen and so I would. It was close enough to Isabel to be aware of her and record things that I needed to.

There are things that I see here, though, that have me wary. I am torn between my duties between being an angel and being the watcher. As an angel, I feel the desire to protect my charge but the Lord has made it clear I'm to record, and nothing more.

It has only been a few times that I've met Father Raphael and yet, he seems familiar. How could that be? His darkness makes my human flesh crawl. Something about him is infinitely evil.

The more time I spent with Isabel and her small circle of what she would call her family, the more I enjoyed my time here. It was a great honor to be asked to record a mortal. It usually meant they were destined for greatness. Some though, would fall into infamy. I wondered idly and with great anticipation, which side of the pendulum my charge would land.

We — the angels I mean, were always curious as to what struck God so much about this particular mortal but we did not question. NEVER did we question his motives. It was an unspeakable act that we learned from when our brother, Lucifer, was cast out of Heaven.

I came to admire Isabel in the short time I was here. I remember looking up from an old man who was just about to pass the threshold of this world to Heaven, lying in the monastery's hospice room bed and seeing Isabel already there.

She knelt beside him, unafraid of the leprosy, and she took his hand in hers and smiled. Silently, she prayed for him, which I heard from her heart. She would laugh and chat with the man so that he was not afraid of being alone.

The frail man stared up into that youthful face of hers which had a natural glow to her skin and eyes. *That was something rare in these times.* Her dark brown hair was often tied back and her white sleeves rolled up as if she were always ready to work, which she was. She laughed easily, allowing the small crinkles of her eyes to deepen and enhance her dark brown irises.

I always thought she was beautiful. There was nothing substantial about her, but there was every reason to stare at her long enough for her to catch you. She was gentle and natural. She was motherly, in a way that made her heart strong and convicted to her mission. She had been known to skip larger portions so that there was always enough for the elderly and sick to eat. I had even seen her take some of her personal blankets down to the children's rooms so that they would be warm while she bundled up in more layers of clothing.

From a very young age this mortal had a love for God and a duty in her soul to serve him. She revealed her intentions to do so, despite the eagerness of the Emperor to have his son marry her. On her own behalf she spoke to Pope Innocent IV and convinced him that her call was to a different life; that of virginity and servitude to the Lord.

Isabel's mother, Blanche of Castile, was known for her powerful influence as a woman of her time and it was clear that her influence rubbed off on both Isabel and her brother. Her death left the siblings in a state of mourning for years, but as a result, the two vowed to stay close and uphold the Queen's pious upbringing.

Even when Isabel was tempted with the hedonistic influences of the court, she remained focused on her calling. She turned down every offer of marriage, even at the urgings of the Pope who also admired and encouraged her vow of purity and servitude to God.

I watched now from my vantage point as Father Dulante gazed across the courtyard at Isabel. She was in the company of the other nuns, smiling at something they were talking about amongst themselves. Dropping his gaze, the priest stared at the words on the pages of his small bible but did not actually read them. His thoughts were elsewhere, thinking about Isabel. She was as beautiful now as she was when he'd known her as a child. His features darkened even as the thought had crossed his mind. This priest prayed nightly to remove her from his heart but now that he found himself the same abbey, called to serve by Father Raphael personally, he questioned how he could ever heal from the boyhood love he felt for her.

As a child, Father Dulante would visit his Aunt Rebecca at

Isabel's home because his mother was often ill. Isabel's family graciously took him into their service, allowing him to stay for long periods of time. The two children would play and run out by the stables where Father Dulante would care for the royal equines. Isabel's horse was a blonde mare named Marigold, given to her when she was old enough to ride alone. He made sure she was groomed daily, fed, and that she was taken care of above all the others.

Once or twice he'd received a good thrashing for doing so because he'd left the other horses unprepared for Louis and his father's early morning hunt. To him, it was worth it. The look of pleasure on Isabel's face when Marigold pranced before her brought light to his life despite the sun.

When Marco was thirteen, his mother died in childbirth from an unexpected pregnancy. His father was unable to care for him any longer and requested that his aunt Rebecca keep him permanently. Rebecca was all too happy to have him. Marco's presence reminded her of her late sister and his work was good enough to keep the stable master content. By permission of Isabel's parents, he was allowed to stay and live with Rebecca, her husband, and her son Edward. It seemed to be the perfect situation to everyone except Edward who was four years older than Marco.

The difference between the two boys was night and day. Marco was even tempered and outgoing where Edward was dark and brooding, even cruel. Where Marco took care of the animals in the stable, Edward joined in the hunting party and took great interest in the skinning and collecting of the kills. On more than one occasion, Marco would wake in the middle of the night to find grimly posed, preserved animals staring at him by candlelight. When Edward was angry with him, the animals were more "fresh" and left in his bed with him.

Even now as the memories came flooding back, Father Dulante's hands began to tremble. One morning, Edward waited for Marco to show up for his chores, hiding in the dark shadows of the stable. When Marco opened the stable door, he noticed that the rope he used to lead Marigold out was missing. Before he was able to turn completely, he felt the rough fibers wrap around his neck and squeeze against his Adam's apple. He tried to scream but the noise was choked off along with most of his air supply in a strict warning. Trembling then, like now, he felt Edward's breath against his ear in a malicious whisper, "Sick little whelp."

Edward hissed and drew the rope tighter until his lips pressed into the soft flesh behind the trapped boy's ear. Marco could feel the danger of consciousness slipping away from him. His teeth began to chatter. Inside his head it was so loud he wondered if they would crack.

“Who invited you here, anyway?” Edward’s words were emphasized with a sudden jerk upward and back of the rope. The motion stole Marco’s balance and he fell to the stable floor but Edward did not allow any give in the rope. In a panic, the smaller boy rolled and twisted, trying to regain his footing but his assailant was already dragging him further into the dark stable like an animal being led to slaughter.

“No!” Marco tried to scream but it was nothing more than a hoarse whisper.

He tried to dig his heels down into the wooden floor and grab for anything to use as a weapon, but taking his hand away from the rope only allowed Edward to pull tighter. Each precious gulp of air was crucial to his survival. So was keeping his wits about him. He was smarter than Edward but Edward was wicked and unstable. Marco had no idea what kind of outcome a match of this kind would bring.

When Edward finally stopped, Marco lay still, trying to control his heart and mind. Edward’s twisted features appeared above him, wielding a rusted blade and waved it back and forth in front of his eyes.

“I’m going to gut you like a dirty pig and hang you to bleed out.” Edward’s voice was cool and even as he spoke the words that rattled Marco’s spine.

Marco’s effort to control his heart rate failed, immediately. The muscle was now pounding so hard he thought his ribs would crack open, allowing it to leap outside his body and leave him to his demise. Without shame, he began to cry and struggle harder, but he was no match for Edward.

Every time Marco managed to make it to his feet, Edward would slam a fist against the side of his head and throw him down to the earth, again. The struggle caused the horses to stir and stomp their hooves against the dense floor. They were throwing their heads back and snorting in agitation. The violence of Marco’s beating made the air thick and heavy with sweat and blood and the animals could taste it.

Marco tried to stand again but his vision was blurry and his eyes were swelling shut. He could see Edward smiling though, and enjoying the infliction of pain. The older boy wanted him to keep fighting. The more Marco fought the more pain Edward would inflict until finally, all his fight would dwindle.

Lying on the dirt floor among the hay, Marco sobbed, knowing he was about to die. Edward began wrapping the rope around his ankles in a silent deliberate way, then moved into his victim's line of vision again. Throwing the other end of the rope up into the rafters, he began to hoist the younger boy's body up until his head swung over the floor by about three feet. Marco's eyes closed when Edward growled, rearing back with his blade. *This is it,* He thought. Edward was about to thrust his blade into the soft part of his younger cousin's belly when Isabel ran from out of nowhere, her arm swung out, and through his impaired vision, Marco watched the older boy's eyes widen before dimming as the light was put out from within.

Edward fell straight to his knees, still holding Marco's gaze before slowly pitching forward and falling to the ground. The hammer was still in Isabel's hand as she stood there, shaking like a leaf. She was staring in disbelief at what she'd done to Edward when Marco's voice finally reached her ears, urging her back to the scene, "Isabel?"

She was still far away but her eyes shifted to his and showed signs of recognition. She had lost all the color in her face. The two were shivering, uncontrollably.

"Please," he said, softly. "Help me down."

Isabel looked around for a way to cut the rope before gazing down with trepidation at Edward's body. He still had the blade clutched within his blood-stained fingers. Her eyes met with Marco's again, and she nearly fell apart knowing she would have to touch the fallen boy to retrieve it but her friend's pleading eyes gave her the strength she'd need. Nodding slowly, Isabel sank to her knees and crawled toward Edward's prone body.

The silence that surrounded them caused every noise she made to be amplified, and any sudden sound provoked them to jump. It seemed that she took an eternity to reach him, and when she did she extended her hand even more slowly toward the blade. Her fingers finally made contact and she let out a breath of relief, then looked up at Marco with a reassuring smile before tugging on it. Confusion set in and her smile faded into terror when she realized that Edward was staring right at her.

"Run Isabel!" Marco screamed.

Isabel scrambled to her feet just as Edward did and both moved to the right, then to the left. Edward's smile was sick and maniacal as he toyed with her. Frantically, Isabel spun and ran back toward the stable door, turning her back on Edward. He used this to his advantage and darted to the other side of the stable out of their line of sight.

The horses were in a fully agitated state, kicking the walls and stomping the floor. Some used their bodies to bump the doors holding them within their stalls. Marco was starting to get lightheaded as the blood continued to rush to his head but he refused to give up. Twisting his body to look any way to get out of this, or see where Edward was, he caught sight of a pair of budnippers on the wall. If he swung hard enough, he might be able to reach them and use them to cut himself down.

It was a slow start but he began. The momentum shifted the world, left then right, and eventually his body was swaying to and fro. His frustration was mounting as he'd come so close to the nippers, his fingertips grazing them before his body would fall away again. He took slow, deep breaths. He needed to relax. He needed to be calm.

In the distance he could still hear the sound of the horses and the scuffling of Isabel and Edward.

"Please God, keep her safe!" he thought. "Just a few more swings."

Isabel rounded one of the stalls and tried to still her breathing. The horse beside her got spooked and jerked away, letting out a small whine. Grimacing, she tried to calm it with her hands but the animal threw its head aside and backed up, throwing her roughly against the wall. Pain sent a spark of white light through the back of Isabel's eyes and she bit her lip to keep from making any noise. She tried to sneak out of the stall and past the horse but Edward was there, waiting for her.

"You're an even better prize than the little pig." He growled.

His hands suddenly gripped her arms like a vice and he drug her to the center of the stable, back toward Marco. Isabel went into a full blown panic, letting out a scream before trying to break free of his grip. Edward's icy smile faded and his features smeared into rage. He raised his hand and sent it crashing down without mercy against her cheekbone. The blow sent the small girl reeling into a spin before she fell to the ground, barely conscious.

"Now, you will pay dearly. I'm going to give you many reasons to squeal." He said, now wrapping her hair around his hand and dragging her through the stable again toward a work table near the back.

Isabel could barely see or walk straight so he shoved her where he wanted her to go. She saw the table and let out a sob. Her futile attempt to push back only made him angrier and he shoved her roughly on top of it, pinning her belly against its surface.

Adrenaline was all the strength that Isabel had left and she tried to fend his attack off as best she could to no avail. Another slap and she watched the blood from her split lip splatter across the wooden table. The sound of metal equipment scraping together behind her made her cry out again. Edward stuffed a dirty rag into her mouth, fingers digging deeply, shoving it into the back of her throat, making the act of breathing nearly impossible. She could feel herself starting to gag as he spun her around, forcing her chin upward so he could stare down at her. She and Marco were the same age, thirteen this year and only months apart. Edward's age and height put him a full foot taller.

"Look at this dirty whore." He leaned down to whisper, allowing his tongue snake along her tear-stained cheek.

Isabel tried to pull back but Edward had her pinned with himself between her legs. He was like an un-moving stone with Hell in his eyes full of malicious intent.

"I see how he looks at you. That little *pig*. Too bad he'll never get to see you again." Edward shoved against her again in a lewd way, and then brought his blade upward, trailing it along her thigh. She could feel the precision of the tip tearing tiny fissures in her skin as it made its trail.

Isabel instinctively jerked back but Edward was unrelenting. He leaned in further, sniffing at her hair until she shook from head to toe and began sobbing through the rag. His hand found home on her breast and squeezed into a claw, his unkempt nails scraped into her skin and drew blood to the surface. Isabel screamed past the restricting cloth and Edward's fury consumed him. His lips curled back over his teeth and he pinned her to the table by her throat, strangling her. Isabel's feet kicked at the air and her fists beat at Edward's arms to no avail. Her eyes were growing darker and darker with each moment of her losing battle when she caught sight of her salvation. *Marco!*

From a far corner, Marco came running and behind him, Isabel saw HIM. *The man with wings.* It all happened like a dream. Edward flew back with a look of surprise and air returned to her lungs. It was a slow return due to the rag being lodged in her throat which she quickly began pulling out of her mouth, but it was enough. Isabel rolled onto her rear and she fell to the floor scooting to a wall as fast as she could while trying to process what she witnessed. Marco was now standing over Edward's body with the shovel still hovering over his head. She could see the inner battle painted on his face. None of it made sense to him. Dropping his weapon, he looked at Isabel who was still staring up at him, but seeing something past him. He turned quickly but saw nothing.

"W-what?! What is it?" He cried out, spinning back to face her.

Isabel just shook her head quickly, and said nothing.

Marco fell to the ground and Isabel scooted back against the wall even further as if she could go right into it. The angel stepped back slowly, pressing his fingers to his lips motioning for silence, and then disappeared. *I'm going mad*, she thought. Closing her eyes, she tried to shut it all out but the light from outside followed by the nursemaid's screams drug her right back into the nightmare.

When Anne couldn't find her this morning, she went searching in the usual places. Isabel was always in the stables with Marigold. What Anne stumbled upon this morning was the horrific aftermath of what these two had just endured. Isabel's entire house was there in a matter of seconds and her father quickly swept her up and out of the mess, carrying her to her room. When Marco's aunt came, he sobbed and reached out for her but she brushed past him, falling to her knees beside Edward. Rebecca's husband and the stable master stood off to the side, exchanging glances.

"What have you done?!" Rebecca spun, laying accusing eyes on Marco.

"He tried to kill me!" Marco cried out. He extended his arms to show the damage that he had suffered at Edward's hands but she did not see.

Rebecca threw herself over Edward, rocking his limp body as she sobbed. Her husband gently pulled at Marco's elbow, "Come on, son. Let's get you cleaned up."

Marco's face was full of confusion and his eyes were soaked in tears. "Uncle? What did I do?"

"Hush, Marco. Come with me." He said, and pulled him again. His eyes told him not to argue and do as he was told.

Even though Isabel had collaborated Marco's story, his aunt was distraught over the death of her only son. The two were questioned for hours well into the night before finally being allowed to clean up and get ready for bed. Marco's body ached from top to bottom and he could barely move as he walked down the hallway to his room. There were whispers from the staff that Edward was "touched by evil" but none would ever speak the words. Saying such things to his mother would cause certain termination of one's job. In her eyes, Edward could do no wrong.

Rebecca's husband on the other hand, was a good man. He tried to buy Marco time but Rebecca was insistent on sending the boy away. She grew more distant and cold with each passing day until Edward's funeral. The day they lay him in the ground Rebecca went into a fit of hysterics, calling Marco a murderer and claiming that she could no longer stand the sight of him. There was nothing more that could be done and Marco's uncle arranged for him to be sent to an orphanage.

When Isabel heard, she burst into her parents' chambers and protested but there was nothing they could do except to ensure that Marco went to a good orphanage and that he was taken care of. Rebecca would not concede to any plea to reconsider, and even left the service of Isabel's family, claiming that the ghost of her son haunted the home.

On the night before Marco was to leave, he sent a gift to Isabel. She watched out the window as his meager, worldly possessions were loaded into the carriage and he stood there with his uncle and her brother Louis. Her eyes filled with tears as she clung to the small locket that he made her. It dangled freely from the braided cord of horse hair that she recognized immediately as Marigold's. The letter attached was penned in his hand:

"Lady Isabel,

Thank you for saving my life. Your family has been like my own, even though I am undeserving of your generosity. God brought me to your door, but briefly. I pray that he shows me the way again, one day. May he love you and keep you in his everlasting light.

Always remember me,

Marco Dulante"

Marco's uncle helped him into the carriage and tousled his hair before stepping back. The boy looked over at his aunt, longingly, one last time but she had already turned and gone inside. He kept a strong face but Isabel could see his shoulders round forward before he turned and sat down. The driver gave a snap of his whip to the horses and the carriage lurched forward.

Isabel ran from the window and threw open her bedroom door. She ran down the stairway and nearly knocked over half the staff as she bolted toward the back the door. Her feet hit the ground and she chased the carriage, running as fast as her legs would carry her. It was no use.

The carriage was growing smaller and smaller as it slipped out of sight, and with it, Marco.

Now, twenty years later, Father Dulante held back the tears of regret. Isabel treated him as if they barely knew one another. It was probably for the best. That day in the stable was a day he did not want to remember either. Edward's eyes still haunted him in his sleep, but most of all he longed to be near her. It was becoming all-consuming. There were days he struggled with it, trying to distinguish whether his faith called him here or if it was some cruel twist of fate that led the way.

Marco realized he'd been staring at the same page for more than just a few minutes and decided to turn to the next. He felt an odd prickling sensation on the back of his neck as if he was being watched. There was plenty of movement in the courtyard that morning but a shadow caught his attention in the distance beyond the crowd. Looking past them, he jumped out of his seat and stumbled back, almost falling over. Between two of the buildings he saw the pale face of Edward peering out at him from under a crimson cowl.

Just as he took a step toward him, he felt a hand on his shoulder and cried out in surprise.

"Father Dulante?" I smiled, even though he could see my confusion. "Are you alright?"

My concern was evident as I gently pulled my hand back.

"Yes." He said, and then looked back in the direction of the buildings for a moment and then seemed to let the thought go. He turned back toward me with a smile. "I thought I saw someone I used to know."

I looked in the direction he did and saw nothing, but I felt it. I knew that whatever he saw was real to him but I did not want to raise alarm, so I smiled and met his gaze again. "It is time for prayers. Shall we?"

I extended my arm forward, motioning toward the chapel and offered him the lead. He seemed grateful at the distraction and nodded, stepping forward with another glance toward Isabel who disappeared into the opposite entrance with the other nuns. His heart was so transparent to me that I felt guilty for knowing what was inside its secret chambers. That guilt was amplified as I met with the deep azure stained glass gaze of the Lord who looked down upon us all as we filed into the chapel. The light that surrounded him warmed my skin as if to reassure me, but the crowd parted and Father Raphael stood alone at the front, replacing Heaven's gaze with his steely, dark eyes.

I made it through prayers even with all the distraction, clutching to the beads of the rosary between my fingers as I prayed for strength and guidance on this mortal plane. I would do all that I could to see through my job as the Lord saw fit. I would record all that I saw, heard, and experienced. No act or moment would slip by without being penned to parchment.

I would soon find out though, that my determination to do God's will would be tested repeatedly. There was darkness afoot. Father Raphael would see to it that things kept me from my duties. I would also find that being a mortal would come with the heavy burden of being tested as one. With mortal flesh came mortal emotions and weaknesses. Prayer was the only weapon I had left to wage war. I was not only gaining more of the mortal emotions and weaknesses, I was losing the memories of my angelic form and home. I could no longer see God's face in my mind. My only connection to the Lord was prayer and his visits.

I was becoming weary and tired. I was aging. I even fell to bouts of sickness. I had no friends, save Father Dulante. I was failing. I needed to do something but I didn't know what that something was.

Recording as much as I could about Isabel was getting harder these days. She had become more of a recluse as time went on. I worried that she might be growing ill from her exposure to the sick, and seeing her today confirmed some of my anxiety. Feeling the need for support, I decided to go watch the boys' choir again. Their voices, so light and innocent, reminded me of Home. It was the best place to be right now. Walking out into the garden courtyard, I caught sight of Isabel wandering through a labyrinth of trees. Smiling at the unforeseen opportunity to observe, I followed her.

The beauty of the garden was that it was a common area. Men and women were allowed to be in the same company. Though speaking for lengths of time would be frowned upon, I could easily sit quietly and feed the birds while keeping vigil over her. I must've been lost in my thoughts and missed a turn she made because I lost sight of her. Turning in circles for a moment, instinct would guide me to the right. It was a more tranquil section of the garden. The foliage was thicker, making the path even narrower. I dipped my hand into the pouch at my waist grabbing some stale bread crumbs from the morning's walk and began to spread them on the grass. Birds were already flocking close to me and the free meal.

Each step I took, I could hear the gravel crunch beneath my weight. The cowl of my robes enveloped my features which made hiding my eyes easier. I could scour the area for Isabel without drawing attention to myself. Pausing for a moment, I listened for any clues of her. The sound of trickling water was close by. Perhaps there was a water fountain? Then the sound of a few crunching footfalls off to my left could be heard before going silent again. I turned in that direction and was about to take a step when a flock of doves fluttered quickly into the sky; a few of them circling the area as if protecting something before flying off again.

Curiosity got the better of me. Isabel could be over there. I proceeded cautiously with my guise at the ready, leaving behind me the trail of bread crumbs. So as to not startle whoever was there, I began to hum softly a song Father Dulante's choir.

As if on cue, a woman's voice chimed in and I smiled, continuing toward it and rounding the corner until I saw her. My smile began to fade when my eyes settled on the woman before me. Isabel was standing there in a strange trance-like state. Her head was tilted back and cocked unnaturally to the side. Staring straight ahead, it appeared that she was captivated by the statue before her. I followed her gaze and saw it. A large angel that was caught mid-flight, his spear aimed at the serpent below him and coiled defensively on the rock. His wings were outstretched in a glorious display, shadowing the sun from the enemy both literally and symbolically. Beneath the rock was the source of the trickling water; it cascaded down into the fountain that I assume, the birds were bathing in prior to her arriving.

As breath-taking as the statue was, I could not understand what held her as transfixed as she was and so before I began to speak, I stood waiting in silence. Other than the sound of the water there was no other sound. No birds singing. No insects buzzing. No breeze rustling through trees. It was completely still. I looked around unnerved by the silence and caught sight of Father Raphael just past the statue in the doorway of a chapel fifty yards away.

In his hand was an apple of which he was carving into with a small, sharp knife. He smiled at me just as he turned, slipping the flesh of the fruit between his lips. Even at that distance the sound of the door to the chapel slamming shut caused me to jump.

The abrupt break in silence shook me to the core until Isabel's voice started to come through, "Marciel?"

It still didn't register, so she repeated my name until I responded.

"Marciel? Can I help you?" She asked.

Blinking, I tried to make sense of everything, "I – No, Milady. I thought I heard someone" I said finally.

She watched me for a moment. I think she was expecting some explanation other than what I had given but whatever I could possibly say would sound mad. It would do me no good to have her against me, especially if I was trying to help her. She looked around as if she were confused on how she got there.

"I don't recall this fountain being here."

"Neither do I, sister" I said.

"Tis very beautiful, is it not?" She mused in a faraway voice.

"Yes, mum. It is." I agreed. And it was. The craftsmanship took on a life of its own. It looked as if the angel might land at any moment.

Isabel's eyes watched me with curiosity for a moment. Something more was behind her gaze but I could not place it. Was it awareness, maybe? Whatever she saw in me, it made me feel self-conscious.

"Are you alright, Milady?" I asked in genuine concern.

She did not seem well at all. Her face had grown pale and slightly gaunt, and a darkness crept around her eyes that I had never seen before. She forced a smile and looked away at the fountain again, remaining silent for a moment before she responded, "I am."

I nodded and gave a slight bow to her, turning to make my way back to my room when she broke in again, "How is your book coming?"

A chill rose up my spine and I could not move. It was Isabel's voice, but it was dark and cold as if it was produced by something or someone else. I turned toward her again, my hands clenching around each forearm beneath the bell sleeves of my robes, "Milady?"

That far away stare was there again. Her eyes were cold and grey for a moment and I awaited her response but one did not come. I was about to repeat myself when her eyes shone with life more and she spoke. It was like having two separate conversations; one she was privy to and one she was not.

“I was just coming out to cut fresh flowers and found myself here” she said. “It’s getting late; I should head back inside before prayers.”

I was speechless for a moment, my jaw hanging loose before I nodded and bowed again, keeping my head low until she passed. It took all my strength of will to remain there and not flee once she had disappeared from sight. If I ran, it would draw attention to myself and attention brought with it questions. I was alone in the garden with Isabel. It could, if someone wanted to portray it in such a way, look less than innocent. I needed help and sound advice.

With a final glance to the chapel I narrowed my eyes searching for signs of Father Raphael then made a quick retreat to the choir room. I needed to be in the company of my Maker, but he was not here. Second to him, Father Dulante was my only hope.

When I found him, Father Dulante stood before the children of the boys’ choir. His frustration was mounting but he always managed to keep level- headed. He was known for his gentle demeanor and ability to mediate tense situations. A handsome man, he was tall for the time standing at six foot three inches. He had a soft, olive complexion and deep brown eyes.

Tapping the podium once more, Father Dulante was calling the attention of the young boys ranging in age from nine to thirteen. Being naturally lean and of good muscle structure, the quiet man often commanded attention from those around him. The boys quieted down and faced the priest who was now brushing back the loose brown bangs that continually fell to his brow when he bent to read the music before him.

Father Dulante was the new young assistant to Father Raphael. His passion was music so the senior priest gave him the task of training the young orphan boys that they often had charge of. He had complained many times before that it was much too cold for the boys to practice in this room. Even with the blazing hearth on the far wall, it was often damp and affected the boys' performance in the early morning. If he was to take his work seriously, he would have to impress upon Father Raphael that it was imperative they get another room.

Despite Father Raphael's cool exterior, he would often come to watch the boys' practice which pleased Father Dulante at first until he noticed a few of the boys seemed on edge at his presence. His lead soprano would often get distracted and his voice would crack or just be off key. He chalked it up to nerves then scheduled a couple more practices with a small audience this upcoming week so that the boy could get used to singing in public.

Isabel once overheard the young priest and Father Raphael in a heated discussion as she passed the room one afternoon. Father Dulante was desperately trying to convince his senior that the boys' voices were too strained in the morning and that their teeth were chattering making the scales close to impossible. She made a mental note to personally see that they received a new room the next day. The children were of a special interest to Isabel. She always made sure they had only the best portions of meals and bedding. A young girl herself when she was led to her calling, she had an affinity for those at such a tender age.

Isabel was not only a child from a noble family, she was also very intelligent. Excelling in education, Latin and easily managed the writings of the Fathers of the Church. She never overlooked more feminine interests such as embroidery but her true delight came from her work with priestly vestments and working for the poor or the sickly.

A devoted daughter and sister, Isabel and her brother, Louis remained close. When Isabel's mother died she founded the Franciscan Monastery of the Humility of the Blessed Virgin. She turned down the abbess, preferring instead to be a humble subject of the Lord. This monastery has been around for nearly nine years since.

Tonight, the women sat around the fire of the small, modest room. The sun was beginning to sink behind the horizon, and the sisters who were already seated watched as Miriam lit the last candle. She turned around, welcoming the last of the congregation inside with a small smile.

The shuffling of shoes and skirts finally died down as Miriam waited to begin her lesson. It was standard practice for each of them to lead one lesson per month. Father Raphael and the Abbess had collaborated on this decision in order to relieve some of the burden from the Abbess. They said that in doing this, it left her more time to focus on other things while giving the nuns more responsibility and keeping their hearts and minds on God.

Isabel looked forward to these lessons, especially when it was Miriam's turn. Miriam was very good at giving lessons and the other women agreed, which made them quiet down and settle even faster, in anticipation. With her bible in one hand and her notes lying gently on her lap, she began with her topic of virtue.

“Our Holy Mother is the standard of our virtue.” Glancing toward the statue of Mary, Miriam paused as if engaged in a silent conversation before turning back toward her audience.

“God called upon our Mother and the apostles to teach us Holy Love, which leads to a virtuous heart.” Miriam leaned forward, setting the book in her lap before letting her eyes sweep over every sister in the front row.

“Each one of them maintained that love and solemn faith through every trial, through every threat, through every danger.” She stopped again, allowing her words to weigh on them then waved her hand flippantly in the air before it found its home on her heart.

“All of them..except *Judas*.” Miriam stood up, suddenly, consumed by the emotion of her message. “Judas allowed the most perfect love and virtue to be corrupted by fear of Mankind. Men who were set upon *murder*! Who wished harm upon the Lamb of God..Our Mother’s *immaculate conception*!”

Every sister now stirred with equal emotion, engaged and entranced with her and shaking their heads. Whispers of disdain filled the room before Miriam straightened up again and turned. Her fingers stretched out widely as she paced like a lawyer pleading his case to the jury. Isabel watched her closest friend but kept her hand pressed against her side to subdue the cramping pain that had begun to plague her since this morning. She would suffer through it in silence out of respect for Miriam. Afterwards, she would make a trip back to the infirmary.

Usually the most quiet and meek of the convent, these lessons brought out Miriam's passion for Christ. Like Isabel, Miriam's decision to join the convent came at a very young age. When most mothers were making deals or contracts, Isabel and Miriam had their eyes lifted to God. A marriage of faith was much more desirable to them than a marriage of convenience. From those early years on, these two girls were nearly inseparable in their service to the convent and the Holy Father.

Turning her attention on Miriam, Isabel watched as the woman became more animated.

"God calls upon us to take our vows deep into our hearts. Our marriage to him goes beyond the mortal realm. We are his brides – his mothers of all that are ill, weary, and less fortunate. We must bring the God-less to his throne. He has chosen us to be the ambassadors of His light and unconditional love. **We** – " She pointed at all those present. Her eyes welled up and her cheeks flushed before continuing with her earnest plea, "are His light in the darkness."

As Miriam continued in her lesson, she was well into the hour that was normally allotted for her time. Isabel's discomfort was growing to a nearly intolerable state. Shifting in her seat again caused one of the sister's to clear her throat in agitation, making Isabel stiffen. She would remain still for as long as she could. There were harsh consequences for interrupting lessons or masses of any kind. Bowing her head, she tried to pray for relief and peace of mind to persevere through Miriam's lengthy sermon.

As she mouthed her final, silent word of prayer, the room began to tilt slightly and Isabel opened her eyes cautiously, picking a place on the floor to stare at. Her hope was that in doing so, it would steady her from the vertigo that was threatening to topple her from her seat.

From the far corner of her eye, Isabel could see the Abbess watching her. The woman's rigid posture amplified the shadow cast upon the wall behind her which flickered and jumped to the light of the candles.

Beads of sweat formed on her upper lip and her eyes grew heavy and hard to keep open. Isabel could feel the temperature of the room spike and the walls spin around her. She gripped the bench beneath her, trying to with all her strength to keep her composure. The nun beside Isabel took her eyes off of Miriam and this caused the Abbess to fly into a fit of rage, knocking the poor girl next to Isabel over.

Isabel felt the first crack of leather sting at her covered flesh and cried out. In a wave of gasps, Miriam stopped and leapt to her feet, then covered her mouth to keep from protesting or interfering; doing so would only serve in them both receiving lashings.

The girls all huddled as close as they could to the surrounding walls. They knew all too well, the fervor in which the Abbess dealt her punishments. According to her logic, there were no accidental lashes; which meant that if you were caught by the snap of a stray lick of her leather, it meant that God saw your hidden transgressions.

For her age, the Abbess lacked no strength in her swing, as Isabel was finding out now. Falling to the floor, Isabel's assault continued even as her consciousness began to slip away. It felt as if she was floating outside her body. Her whimpers and cries of pain to each resounding snap against her skin came from further and further away.

The room lurched again and she was suddenly back inside her own stinging flesh being carried by the others in a rush to the infirmary. Isabel vaguely remembered Miriam's cry for the Abbess to show mercy.

"Mother!" She shouted.

"Mother, please! She's bleeding!" Miriam screamed and pointed to the growing red stain at Isabel's side.

Even then the Abbess seemed to debate her relent of that final blow as her arm hung in the air. The frigid glare of the tall, imposing frame of the woman above Isabel's writhing form kept all the nuns clinging to one another until her arm re-cocked at her side. A half-breath later, the women moved like a flock, swooping in to rescue their fallen sister. Lifting her wispy frame, the nuns rushed her down the dark, cold hallway and down the stairs to the infirmary. Little did anyone know, it was here that Isabel would be spending a lot more of her time.

It was here that I watched as the women crowded Isabel, their hands patting and caressing her trembling limbs in meager attempts of soothing her agony. I pressed back against the wall to try blending in and fend off any unwanted attention. It worked for now.

I slid against the stone, moving back to the task I had been tending to before the interruption. I hung my head low; it helped to hide some of my height. Keeping my ear toward the door, I dipped the cloth into the hot water of the basin and wrung it out. The filth of the sick man before me bled into the clear water. I stared into it for a long moment before the limp hand next to me twitched to some fever induced nightmare.

Steam rolled off the cloth as I began to wipe down his arms and neck. The stench of decay already filled the room despite my every effort to keep him, and it clean. Part of my daily tasks were to scrub the stone floor with boiling water, keeping as much infection away as I could. Despite all my efforts though, the Black Death would take them; their eyes would grow hollow and sink back, and their mouths would grow slack and hang, allowing their souls to float out.

"Help me." He croaked.

I shook my head to bring myself back to the present, and looked down at the man lying before me. His grey hair was stuck to his skin, matted beneath the weight of his head and drenched in sweat. Leaning forward, I pressed my hand against his forehead gently before letting my lips make contact with his salty, clammy, damp skin.

"I'm just the Watcher." I whispered.

His eyes grew sad. He Knew. With my words, came the confirmation of what I was and what his outcome would be. Tears fell from his old eyes and he sobbed in silence. All I could do was kneel beside him and speak comforting words. Interfering was forbidden.

"Peace to you, child" I said, pretending to lead him into prayer, "Your Angel comes. And with him, your salvation."

It wasn't long before the man released his last breath. With it, his head grew heavier and I slowly lowered it to the cot beneath him. There was no angel to escort him. He was alone, with no one to lead him out of this world but me. The thought overwhelmed me so much so that I wept quietly while holding his fragile, lifeless hand in my own.

There was bustling, movement, and tending to Isabel in the other room, which was good. She was, at the very least, alive. No one came in to check on this man for many hours. It became my personal duty to finish cleaning him so that he would have a dignified death, and to tidy his sheets. Allowing him to lie in his own filth was something I could not do. The anger seeped in again as the shadows of the room grew longer and night crept in. Where *was* his angel? He did not emanate evil, so why was it he was not escorted Home?

I had to get out of there. I slid my hand from the skeletal cradle of the dead man's and walked swiftly out to the fresh night air. Pacing back and forth, I could not contain my emotion and headed out toward the path leading to the garden.

Plagued by all of these mortal thoughts I was suddenly joined by the Lord at my side. He took on his human form and fell into step with me. At the realization of his presence I abruptly pause and begin to kneel when I feel his warm hand on my shoulder.

"Do not kneel Marciel, lest you draw attention to us." The lord spoke quietly in my ear and when I looked at him there was that same gentle smile on his features which always warmed my heart.

"Yes, my Lord."

I continued to walk alongside him until we were far from the main house. He paused and I did too, and turned to look into his eyes. The Lord stared back into mine; something no mortal could ever withstand. His eyes saw *everything*. Every dark corner of your soul was an open book to him. There was never anything unturned. Even to an angel like me it could be overwhelming.

"Your soul is troubled Marciel. Speak to me and tell me what it is."

I could only follow along and give in to his request obediently. He sat down on a large stone and opened his robe, then pulled out and unwrapped a small loaf of bread. I could smell the sweet dough on the breeze now and I smiled. Sitting down on the ground, I looked up at him sighing quietly to clear my thoughts.

"I feel an evil presence around the monastery."

The Lord did not speak. He broke the bread and handed me a piece, keeping his eyes on mine which urged me to continue.

"Father Raphael– There is something.." I paused, trying to find the words.

"Familiar?"

"Yes." I said. "But how could that be?"

The Lord only smiled and ate a piece of his bread. I took a piece of mine and ate with him. We were silent for a long moment before the Lord finally broke the silence.

"There are things that are not your concern. Your Father in Heaven knows all things. Trust him. Obey his command. That is your only concern Marciel. Let the Father take on the burden of worry."

I felt an instant warmth and relief to his words like something washing over me cleansing the dirtiness of the wicked I felt. I do not know if it was him banishing the worry or if his words actually caused me to let go. But somehow, I felt better and the burden lifted off my shoulders. I could breathe again, and laugh. I felt a longing to be in Heaven once more, but I felt too ashamed to voice the words. So instead, I spoke of all the wonderful things I'd learned during my time on Earth.

We finished off the rest of the night with talk of other things. When the Lord left me, I prayed. I asked the Father to guide me and for strength to follow my task then stood and headed back to the main house.

CONDEMNATION - MARCIEL

When I arrived, there was a rush of people walking in and out of the front door. Confusion was high as I watched the faces of those that passed me. I stopped and asked one of the men what was wrong and he shook his head, pulling his arm from my grasp. I looked upward into Isabel's window and saw in the candlelight behind the half drawn curtain, the silhouettes of a couple people bustled back and forth.

My first instincts were to run with unnatural speed, or to push my wings through the frail human flesh, to fly like the wind to her, my charge. Without my wings, I couldn't do that. I was just a human, to them. All I knew was that something was horribly wrong. I knew it instinctively. I made my way through the crowd to see Isabel being held against her bed. She appeared to be convulsing and the smell of jasmine was so strong it that I nearly choked on it. The crowd that gathered around her whispered among themselves and I shoved through them until I was standing bedside.

Father Dulante looked up at me. The worry on his face caused my heart to sink. I turned to look down on Isabel again and saw that there was blood everywhere. Panic rose up in me and I felt helpless.

"What do I do?" I yelled. The more she flailed, the more those crimson droplets flung onto the vestments of the priests holding her down.

"She's having a seizure!" cried Miriam.

"Strap her down!" yelled Father Raphael, who now shoved his way forcefully through the crowd.

It was an instant sickly feeling that overcame me. My body pitched forward and I knew he was there before he even opened his mouth to speak. I spun around and came face to face with the priest whose eyes were dark and cold as they stared down at Isabel. The pitch darkness of his eyes was a void and looking into them was the equivalent of falling into the pit of Hell, itself. I had to get away from him. With all the commotion it wasn't easy but I managed to pull back and get to a safe distance. The two nuns who were standing off to one side, looked at one another as if doubting Father Raphael's orders but quickly moved to obey them. They came back carrying two leather cuffs attached to straps that were used for some of the mental patients or surgical patients that they had to tend to. Working silently, the two women shackled Isabel's biceps and ankles down.

Once Isabel was cleaned, we could see the wounds were on her wrists. I felt the world spin around me. These wounds were too perfect. Grasping her hand gently in my own, I turned it to get a better look. There was one on each wrist in the space bound by the hamate, the triquetrum, the lunate, and the capitate. It is said that only those few that experience true stigmatic symptoms receive the wounds in the correct location. The excitement around me became muted, and like a distant pulse Father Dulante's voice came through the pounding of my heart in my ears.

"Marciel!" he shouted, grabbing my attention.

"What? Yes? Sorry." I stuttered.

"Bandages, please?"

I turned on a heel, disoriented and dazed. This was a new sensation for me. I didn't know what to do. My path seemed unclear once more. I ran for the hospice room and grabbed the bandages. On my way past the kitchen I also took a bowl with some clean water and jogged back to Isabel's room. I nearly dropped the bowl at the vision before me as I came to her doorway. Father Raphael was sitting beside her, staring into her face with a cold, empty smile. It disappeared as soon as I could focus my eyes again and the priest looked up at me.

His hand lifted and fingers curled inward, beckoning me to come near. My knuckles whitened as the grip I had on the bandages and the bowl tightened. It was a struggle for me, being what I am, to come near such a vile creature. I knew in my pure heart there was only blackness in his.

Father Raphael looked like an average man. He stood at about 5 foot 9 inches and so I had to look down at him as he spoke which seemed to agitate him even further. His long black hair was always impeccably tied back and neat. Ironically, he had an angelic complexion, fine and beautiful, like a painting. To look at him, one could fall into his dark eyes if they were not aware of the evil permeating within.

He was an older man of about maybe forty or fifty years. It was hard to tell. When his hand touched my shoulder I had to restrain from jerking back. The evil inside him burned my skin and caused me great pain. Flesh beneath the cloth sizzled and blistered so that I could no longer speak, lest I give it away. When he leaned in, I could smell the thick sulfur rolling off his malicious whisper.

"I know you watch me." He said.

I tried to swallow and shake my head. Did he know? No. It was impossible. Wasn't it?

"What do you mean, Father?" I managed to stammer out.

Father Raphael only smiled and I felt his hand lift from my shoulder. I closed my eyes for a moment as he stepped behind me to get my bearings again and was immediately brought out of it by his voice hissing in my ear once more.

"Know your place." It said.

I felt my breath stretch my lungs and I realized I had been holding it but not before a whisper was quickly added to that last warning.

"Angel." It hissed out slowly and I thought my ears drums were on fire.

I spun around but he was gone. I imagined it. I had to. It was impossible for him to know my secret. To know God's secret! I heard Isabel moan and I left those thoughts behind to tend to her.

As I dipped the clean rag into the water I kept looking over my shoulder before wiping the blood from Isabel's skin. Fear was not something angels knew in Heaven, but here on Earth, I did. I was panting when I felt Isabel's hand touch mine. I let out a small, choked out yell and caught myself. Wiping my brow with the back of my hand, I laughed and smiled looking down at her. Giving her hand a squeeze to try and reassure her, I shrugged sheepishly.

"I'm jumpy tonight. I thought we'd lost you." I said.

It wasn't a lie. I don't think I could've pulled off a lie right now to save my own wings.

"How long have I been out?" she asked.

"Six hours."

She seemed so lost. I wanted to wrap her up in my arms and keep her safe but I knew that I couldn't. Lowering my eyes to the rag again, I continued my task of cleaning and bandaging her wounds.

Isabel moved to sit up quickly but was stopped by the leather binds. A look of confusion was quickly filled in with a look of anger then hurt. She tipped her head to the side and leveled her gaze at me as if trying to read me and figure out was I the one who tied her up.

"No, it wasn't me. Father Raphael ordered it. You – you were having a seizure." I said but I knew it was a lie.

"I demand you untie me. Untie me at once!" she was starting to grow irate the more she pulled at the binds and the more she could not free herself.

The shouts brought back the nuns who rushed in and to her side. The two sisters urged her to lie down and rest.

"Rest, dear" the one said while the other chimed in.

"Yes, Isabel, you've had a long day. Rest and get your strength back."

"I'm not resting until you untie me!" Isabel demanded once more.

Father Raphael was suddenly at the door. My hand squeezed tightly around the rag dripping into the water. The two nuns stood upright instantly and lowered their eyes in silence. Isabel stopped and watched them, brows furrowing before turning toward Father Raphael again.

"What is this?" she asked.

"Untie her. She is no harm." Said Father Raphael with an air of disregard, and then he disappeared around the corner, again.

The two nuns worked on each side of the weak woman to free her. Isabel pulled her arm away from them and rubbed out the pain with a wince. The two women looked at each other, then me, before slipping out into the hall without a word.

I could feel the anger welling up in Isabel. I knew that it was aimed at Father Raphael. Just as I would speak, Father Dulante entered and I could hear his sigh of relief.

"Isabel. You're alright." He said.

Her smile was weak but bright, none the less. Father Dulante sat on the edge of her bed, offering her a cold cup of fresh water.

"I bet you're thirsty. Are you hungry at all?"

Isabel took the mug and drank it, savoring the water like a fine wine before she answered.

"I'm starving!"

We all laughed and I stood up to excuse myself. I had much to write tonight. I had almost forgotten that I needed to record this event. With a hasty, fumbling apology, I picked up the dirty rags, bandages, and the soiled water then retreated down the corridor toward the kitchen. Out of the corner of my eye, I saw Father Raphael slip back into his room.

I slammed the bowl down onto the kitchen's heavy table and caused two of the workers to jump. The surface of the table cracked. I know they heard it but I didn't care. I'm sure I was the lesser of their worries with Father Raphael lurking in shadows and dark corners. I muttered another apology and headed to my chambers, dropping the rags off in the laundry heap on the way.

As soon as I was inside my room, I fell down on my knees. Clasping my fingers together tightly I looked up into the moonlight that shone through the small window and prayed fervently. I wept the words, pleadingly.

"Father, please! Please grant me the strength to do thy bidding. Banish this fear from my weak soul. Give me the wisdom to make the right decisions. Guide me through this. I am but a humble servant, Lord."

The tears fell from my cheeks and I leaned forward, pressing my face to the cold stone of the floor. I stay that way for hours, letting the salty tears form a puddle under my lips and nose.

I heard nothing. No response to my plea. No comfort to my despair and my fear. It was as though I had been forsaken. I looked around and saw the shadows retreat, hissing and recoiling to the cracks and crevices, alive with some kind of life of their own. I threw myself back and crashed into the side of the bed, breaking the leg and stumbling down onto the mattress. I felt a hand on my shoulder and was about to run when I heard the Lord's voice.

"Marciel." He whispered.

"Oh, God!" I spun around and fell to my knees, clutching his robe with my fists.

His eyes stared down at me, soothing me with that warm smile. I could feel him lift me to my feet but I was still sobbing and curling inward like a small child. I felt safe in his arms and did not want to leave the sanctuary that they were. I was shaking, I could feel it. I had never felt so many human emotions all at once. I felt pity for them that they had to endure this.

"Be strong, Angel. The Lord is here with you." His words fell gently to my ears.

"I have fought many evils Lord but this evil" I stammered, "this evil is overwhelming. Is it because of the human body I hide in? Speak to me, Lord. Please!"

The Lord brushed his hand over my brow like a father to his son, smiling brighter. I suddenly felt like a child afraid of the boogie monster in the closet and the heat of embarrassment filled my face. He led me to my writing table and pulled out the chair with his free hand. His arm that was around me, gently guided me to sit and then he handed me the quill.

"Write, Marciel. That is all you must know. Just, write." He said.

I was stunned. What about this mortal? What about me? Was this evil strong enough to destroy me? With all the wars I had fought, I now felt like a child fighting off a nightmare. I felt alone and scared. The fear made me feel foolish and now he was guiding me to write? I stared down at the quill and watched as the tip shook in my trembling hand not from fear but from the internal struggle.

How could I sit here and do nothing? Because it's God's will. Why was it God's will to let this mortal be prey to such evil? Just write.

The thoughts mulled around in my mind and I fought to keep control. I kept reminding myself of what the consequences were of testing God's will. I kept forcing myself to remember what God did to –

I froze. Oh, God, it can't be.

"It's Lucifer, isn't it?!" I spun around to ask but the Lord was gone.

MARCO DULANTE: WORLD IN MY EYES

Marco, sighed at the sound of Isabel's laughter. Even in her weakened state it was music to his ears; and music was the one thing that mended Marco's heart when he left Isabel's family for the boys' home five hundred miles away. When he arrived there, he and his caretaker were received with peaceful smiles and generous offerings. They showed Marco and his companion for this trip, to a large room with all the comforts he'd grown accustomed to in his former home. He had some hope that life might not be so bad for him.

A week later, when Marco watched his companion leave, he was quickly introduced to the way life would *really* be. It was still dark on a Thursday morning. His door flung open and the burly man in charge, whom all the children called Monsieur, barked at him.

"Wake up, worthless goat dung!"

Marco blinked a few times, and Monsieur grew angry. It was Marco's first lesson in the large man's temper, which he swore from that day on, never to invoke again if he could help it. The crack of his rod brought with it the searing pain and the rise of his skin in a thick, red welt.

Scrambling to get to his feet, Marco stood there in the half-light, wide-eyed and shivering with cold, "Sir, please. What ..what did I do?"

The large man wobbled toward him, waving the rod to emphasize his threatening tone, "Your days of leisure are over! You belong to me and from now on you will earn your keep!"

He was bellowing so loudly that his face transformed to a beet red color. His jowls wiggled like gelatin and his eyes grew bloodshot with each shout and frantic wave of his arm. Marco continued to back up until he felt the cool, stone wall behind him. Monsieur finally stopped yelling and pointed out the doorway.

"You sleep with the other fodder." He sneered with contempt, and when Marco didn't respond fast enough, he began shouting again, "Go! Go now, boy!"

Marco ran past him, crouched low and fearful of the rod's sting reaching him again. Once he was all the way out of the room and half way down the hall at a safe distance, he turned. The staff were removing all of his things by the box full. He was dumbfounded. Everything he'd ever had, had been lost or stolen from him. Curling within himself, he turned back around and headed toward the communal bunks with the rest of the boys.

The morning had just broke light and began to filter in by the time he was awakened for the second time. The bustle and commotion of the other boys got him set into motion. Getting dressed in the plain grey uniform tunic and robes, they were all given, he followed the rest down to the breakfast room.

There were boys that were taller much older than he was who reminded him of Edward, and he cringed subconsciously. They pushed past him and the smaller boys roughly, ensuring they'd get the larger, better portions of what little food was served. The smaller boys did not protest. Instead, they all backed up and gave the older boys more room.

Marco fell into a state of despair. He went through the motions slowly, hoping to fit in well enough that he would blend in with the walls and avoid attention all together. One of the friars entered and began ringing a large bell. Clanging it loudly, he shouted over the calamity.

"Let's go! Clean up! Time for lessons!" Each shout was followed by another, hard clang of the large bell.

Marco followed the boys until they came to another room. They all began filing in, once more brushing past Marco as he stood there watching. A tall, slender man who almost looked like a woman stood in the center of the room. The boys surrounded him and stepped onto the risers: shorter ones up top, taller ones staying on the floor. When the man turned around, Marco took a visible step back. His dark eyes were made even darker by the paint that he wore on the lids. If that weren't frightening enough, he had a gaze that would go right through you like a spear. Slowly, he let that gaze fall onto Marco.

"You are new." He said, staring down his angled nose at him.

Marco hated the weight of this man's stare. It was heavy and judgmental, and felt as cold as a winter's day on him.

"Yes, my Lord." Marco responded in barely a whisper.

"I am Maestro Arasorio." He said, and straightened up his long, twisted spine with vanity and pride.

As if he wasn't frightening enough, he extended a waif-like hand and pointed off to the side, "Stand over there and listen."

“When you feel like you understand your *place*, find your way to proper riser.” He instructed, and then continued.

“If you take too long I will assume you do not wish to praise our glorious Father, and I will send you off to Monsieur…” He paused then and lifted is pencil thin brows before leaning in closer “For adjustment.”

Marco decided right then and there that he had no idea what that meant, and he had no intentions of finding out, either.

“Yes, my Lord.”

The man took an extra-long moment to pull his gaze away from Marco and re-focused on the crowd in front of him. Raising his hands upward, his spindly body poised awkwardly frozen in that moment while every one of the boys’ eyes locked on him. Maestro Arasorio swayed with a sudden lurch to the side, sending his curly hair thrashing about but what he commanded and pulled from that seemingly flamboyant and ungraceful movement was a singular rise of voices. The boys’ voices fell into unison and created such a heavenly sound that Marco released a sudden, small gasp.

The voices were light and angelic. The sound made keeping his eyes open any longer impossible. Lulled into a trance, Marco's eyelids fell shut and he was lost in blissful rapture. Each one of those boys alone, were nothing more than he was. All of them were the discarded trash, abandoned by the rest of the world. Together however, their voices commanded the soul, and brought the voices of angels down to earth.

From that day onward, Marco dedicated his life to music and to God. It was only God who could've known what his heart needed. Music spoke to him straight from the Father's lips to his ears, and he knew it was the only thing that could replace the hole left there by Isabel's absence. He threw everything he was into learning the hymns and the music. Eventually, he even earned favor with Maestro and Monsieur. When people heard Marco sing, they requested the boys' choir more often and the word spread from each house of nobility to the very halls of the Vatican.

One summer afternoon, word from Rome came. The pope requested the presence of the boys' choir and specifically, Marco. Monsieur's eyes lit up with gold coins. It was Maestro who brought the subject up of what they would wear.

"Monsieur! You cannot go before the Holy See with the boys in such condition!" He exclaimed, his eyes stretched wide at such a ridiculous notion.

"You expect me to spend all my earnings on these goat fodders?!" He yelled back.

"I cannot work this way." Maestro threw his hands up and sauntered away and then rushed back again in a fit.

"You expect too much, Monsieur! It is a performance before the Pope. Head of the Catholic Church! He can take the boys away from you as easily as scratching his nose!" Maestro's voice had hit a glass-shattering soprano pitched shriek.

Monsieur scoffed and pushed the Maestro away, throwing his frail body against the doorway, "Not one pence more than what is needed, or I'll shove my dagger so far into your arse you'll speak of shit for weeks!"

Maestro cried out at the threat then maneuvered past the large man, scurrying like a rat along the stone to make the arrangements.

When the boys woke up the next morning, they went into the music hall and were greeted with miles of fabric. Velvet and damask, golds, and reds at every turn. Women were already working to cut patterns and pulling the boys off to the side for measurements. In one corner they measured for jackets, in another for pantaloons and still another for slippers.

When the storm was finally over, the boys looked at one another and burst into laughter. There was pushing and rough housing as they teased each other before the sound of Monsieur's rod snapped them into order.

"If any of you little bastards rips or soils these outfits I shall rip your young testicles from between your legs and feed them to the swine in the yard!" He hissed from between his rotted teeth.

Jabbing the end of the rod into each of the older boys' faces, then swinging it around to encompass them all, he assaulted them with the foulest threats Marco had ever heard. And they knew, he'd follow through with each one if their outfits did not come back just as pristine as when the boys left.

The boys were undressed and washed. Even Marco didn't recognize his own reflection when he gazed into the mirror. Not only did he look and feel human again, he *smelled* human. He couldn't help but smile. He was sixteen now, nearly a man. His jaw was starting to square off and his body was lean and strong from manual labor. He managed to take in enough nourishment to not look sickly, but not too much that he would be noticed for gluttony. Looking down at his hands, his smile grew more. Even his nails were clean.

The older maids came in to dress them and do final touches to the outfits before their first performance. The travel to get here was long and arduous but the beds and linens that the Pope arranged for them to sleep in the night before felt like he was sleeping in the clouds. There was a knock on the door and Maestro snapped his fingers, commanding his troops' attention.

"Shh! Shhh!" He sounded like a snake.

The boy at the door spoke in a soft, gentle tone. "The Pope calls for you and Marco Dulante. He wishes to have a private audience with you before your performance during mass."

Spinning dramatically, Maestro's long fingers beckoned Marco toward him. When Marco looked surprised and faltered, Maestro snapped his fingers, again. His face twisted into a contorted mask.

"Move quickly, boy!" He whispered loudly.

Marco rushed toward him and lowered his head, obediently. Dark curls fell to his brow but he peered from under them to look past the boy at the door. The Vatican was adorned in every luxury imaginable and it made Marco's jaw go slack. With a pinch from Maestro, Marco flinched but submitted without another sound.

"Please boy, lead the way."

Then Maestro's grip on Marco's elbow tightened and he pulled the boy closer, whispering into his ear, "If you mess up, I'll feed you to Monsieur and his seedy men back home. You'll know the meaning of fodder by the time they are through with you. Do you understand? Just nod if you do."

Marco nodded quickly and Maestro plastered his fake, jester-like smile onto his face greeting everyone they were introduced to before a clergy of men in white and crimson robes marched forward, the Holy See in the middle of them all. The papal group moved past them all as they lowered beneath the shortest one, reverently. The Pope stopped before his chair and turned. The others followed his movements. When he sat, they did, too.

In an old, gravelly voice, the Pope beckoned for Maestro who made an like exaggerated boy and leaned in to kiss the holy ring.

"So this is your apprentice, Antonio?"

Marco watched intently, brows rising at the familiarity between the Pope and the Maestro. The Maestro only bowed further before speaking.

"Since my infraction upon you, I have crawled into the deepest, foulest bowels of the Devil's cesspool to find a thing of beauty..." Maestro said, then looked up at the old man from beneath hooded, painted lids, "For *you*."

Lifting his twisted spine so that he was erect again, he stepped back and let his hand present the boy who'd nearly died at Isabel's home, now dressed and elevated to the privilege of meeting the Pope.

Marco bowed low seeing that the Holy Father had let his eyes move from Maestro to himself. The priest was about to speak to the boy when another man stepped up and leaned in to whisper against the Pope's ear. Marco could see from the corner of his eye, the gnashing of teeth from Antonio Arasorio, the discarded Maestro of the Pope.

The gravel-torn voice of the Father reached them, once more, "Maestro, I don't doubt that he's every bit as beautiful as you declare him to be. Will you both wait for me here, I have a small matter to attend to."

Maestro was about to protest but the quick shot of the Pope's eye put him into place without another word. The Priest lifted his hand then and waved the small audience at the door to come in. What Marco saw next nearly stopped his heart. Isabel was being escorted by her mother and father, along with another boy around his age and what appeared to be his parents. His heart was growing heavy like lead with each step she made toward them. She seemed sullen and morose, nothing like the girl he remembered playing with. It all came flooding back. Edward had stolen their innocence in every way, that day.

He could bear no more and turned to look away, tightening his jaw in anger and hurt. He understood now. She was about to be betrothed and they were seeking the blessing of the Holy See.

"Isabel, Louis!" The Pope's graveled voice turned softer, almost grandfatherly.

Isabel and Louis bowed, both taking turns kissing the Pope's ring. Her parents made their greeting, and so did the other young man and his.

"George." He said, finally. "I haven't seen you since you were born, at your christening."

Marco felt the eyes on him and he tried with all his might not to look but he could not stand it anymore. Turning his head, his eyes met Isabel's and she looked as shocked to see him as he was when she walked in. The conversation turned in her direction again and she drug her gaze away to participate. As he feared, they were discussing the conditions of Isabel's engagement.

"However, your grace…" Isabel's mother said, turning to look at her daughter. "Our Isabel feels it is her duty to serve God, before man. She prays that you grant her to be excused from her betrothal to commit to the duties that God has called her to."

Marco's heart skipped a beat and looked up from the floor toward the two women, then over at George who seemed to want no part in any of the arrangements. He did not love her! He could care less if they were betrothed or not. For a split second, he had hope but it was drowned out by the conversation of Isabel's servitude and vow to chastity and servitude. She'd rather be a nun than to marry this boy.

After hearing the arguments, the Pope deliberated before asking to speak to the two alone, without either set of parents. Taking the two into another room, it was nearly an hour before he emerged again.

"Rarely, have I ever seen a commitment so embedded in a soul as I have seen with Isabel. She truly has the calling of God. God's command speaks above men in all things." He gazed at both parents in strict warning of contesting his decision before turning to Isabel. "I grant you pardon from your betrothal, under the condition that you be handed over to the care of Abbey of your parent's choice."

George's parents were seething with anger but acquiesced all the same. Giving a curt bow, they turned and stormed out of the court. With a bemused smile, the Pope watched them before turning to Isabel and her family.

"You must stay for mass. This is Maestro Antonio Arasario and his apprentice, Marco Dulante. They will be accompanying the sermon with their music."

Isabel smiled and turned to her parents, "We must. It is a sign."

She turned back toward the Pope and leaned forward again, pressing her lips to his ring, "God bless you, Father, for all your kindness."

Marco saw the gift he'd made for her capture the light from the stained glass windows. Their eyes met again and he saw the acknowledgment. God take his soul, he would sing for *her* today. He would sing louder and with more spirit than ever before, so that she could hear him, and him alone even among the others.

POLICY OF TRUTH - MARCIEL

I sat that night, thinking of what to write. The more I sat there, the more I thought. The more I thought, the less I could focus, and the more my emotions took over. The quill shook in my hand. Finally, I broke the tip against the parchment and ink bled in a small pool, then absorbed into the porous surface. Throwing my arm across the top of the desk, I shoved everything onto the floor and then dropped my head to my forearm as it lay on the edge.

I heard a knock at my door and I sat up abruptly thinking it was Father Raphael. Closing my eyes, I tried to will it all away but the knock came again, a little more urgently. Standing up, I crept to the door and whispered at the crack between the frame and the door itself.

"Who is it?"

"Father Dulante. Marciel, are you alright? I heard a crash."

I breathed a sigh of relief and opened the door, smiling at the young priest before opening it completely to allow him inside.

"Come in. Yes, I'm alright. Just – just writer's block." Again, it was not entirely a lie.

Father Dulante entered and looked around, turning to face me once more. For a moment he was silent as if he were sizing up the situation then let out a laugh. He shook his head and moved toward the desk to help clean up the mess.

"I never would've guessed that you had outbursts, Marciel. You seem so calm all the time."

"I could say the same of you, Father Dulante." I smiled as I knelt beside him, picking up the parchment bleeding with black ink.

Father Dulante made me feel comfortable and safe. Not in the same way the Lord did, of course, but he had an air about him that made it seem as though everything would just be alright in the end. He had such a pleasant smile and a soft voice. It was deep but not intrusive to one's ears. It was soft and lulling, like a quiet song.

He was also very intelligent. I often overheard his practice sermons or him counseling another member of the monastery. He was wise beyond his years but it was also his peaceful soul that set people at ease the same way it did mine.

I stood up and thanked him for his help then offered him a drink of wine to settle and unwind after such an eventful night. He readily accepted and we sat near the window, talking by moonlight of many things.

I let him do most of the talking. He told me of his calling to priesthood and how he met Father Raphael. I did my best to keep my feelings unreadable to him. If he knew, he did not say or respond. Father Dulante was also a very polite man and very proper. He, too, came from a noble family.

His speech was plain and yet still elegant at the same time. He could speak Latin fluently as well as Italian, French and Portuguese. Education was important to him, but his passion was music. He said that it soothed even the most unsettled soul. To him it was a language anyone could speak fluently and understand.

To hear him talk brought me much joy. I could listen to his stories all night long. I learned that his full name was Marco Dulante. I said the name over and over in my head, loving how it was so fluent like everything else about him.

The night was starting to pull back and he stood, frowning a bit. I thought perhaps my silence offended him and stood with him.

“I’m sorry. Did I offend you, Father Dulante? I was just enjoying your stories so much.” I offered.

“No, no. It is just late and I remembered I have a meeting with Father Raphael in the morning to go over the sermon for my first mass.”

I must not have hid my disdain so well this time. Father Dulante laughed quietly again and let his hand rest on my shoulder. It took all I had to not wince. He patted the same spot where Father Raphael’s handprint was now burnt into my flesh.

“He is not so bad once you get to know him my friend. He is just” the priest paused as he thought of a good word or description, “Well, I don’t know what he is, but he’s not all bad. God makes all kinds.” He smiled as he said it and I could not help but mirror his smile.

I walked my new friend to the door and waved goodnight to him. I wanted to follow him and walk him safely to his door but I did not want him to get the wrong impression. Instead I closed my own door and leaned my back against it hoping I could hear his footsteps and the sound of the handle to his door.

I lost track around the last twenty-five steps and bit my lip. I vowed that I would walk past his door in about twenty minutes to check on him. The back of my head hit the door softly before I pushed myself off of it and headed back to my desk. I sat down in the chair and ran my fingers through my hair.

It was thick and blonde, like a summer's sun. Like Father Raphael, I had an angel's complexion; fair and glowing. Blessed with eyes as blue as God's sky and the vision of a majestic eagle, I also had supernatural hearing.

I was pleasing to look at, I decided, as I looked into the mirror above my desk now, but I was still a stranger to myself. There were no wings, no golden chest plate, no golden sword. I didn't know who I was looking at half the time.

Just as I was about to look down I saw a figure behind me and I jumped forward, knocking my chair over to turn round and round. I reached for that golden sword that was not there. Neither was the figure.

I couldn't handle this, so I made up my mind to go sit with Isabel. Word buzzed around the Monastery that her brother was coming to visit her and should be arriving tomorrow. This was good news to me. Her brother was very strong and brave. He would let no harm come to her.

I listened to Isabel speak so fondly of her brother, Louis, who succeeded Louis VIII. He was renowned for the prosperity and peace he brought his subjects. He had even been captured at al-Mansurah and ransomed but remained in the Holy Land to strengthen the fortifications of the Christian colonies.

Louis doted on his younger sister. The two were quite close and shared many talks about current events or his travels. She would share some accomplishments she'd made with the poor and sickly and then the two would dine together before Louis set off again.

Tonight though, Louis was riding hard to reach his sister who he was told was very ill. Arriving earlier than expected, the servants rushed to greet the man as he brushed past them to his sister's room. His responses to their elated greetings were polite but curt and I followed quickly behind the bustling crowd as they tried to take his coat and offer him wine.

He had just reached the stairs and turned around, waving them all off exasperatedly. Shooing them into the shadows they crawled out of.

“I’m fine! I will be in Isabel’s room. If you wish to serve, have my dinner prepared and brought there.” He went to speak again and we heard the screams. Louis’ companion shadowed him, followed by me and about twelve other servants to the source of it. The closer we came to Isabel’s room, the louder it became.

Louis’ companion drew his weapon as he flanked his Lord closely. It was apparent that his main duty was to protect Isabel’s sibling. The man was nearly as tall as I was with long blonde hair such as mine. His eyes were large and a striking color of green like I’ve only ever seen in nature in the Garden of Eden. I could smell battle on him, it was in his veins and I could tell that he was a seasoned warrior and probably why Louis kept him so close.

Louis got to her door and went to open it but the handle wouldn’t budge. It was locked from the inside. He stepped back and after the split second moment of shock, he quickly threw his shoulder against the door. It was futile but he would not give up and soon, his companion and I both joined in.

“Isabel!” he cried out. “Isabel, it’s me Louis, open the door!”

There was no answer and panic was rising in the three of us. Two more times of us hurling our full weight at the door and it splintered on its hinges and slammed against the wall. Louis stumbled inside and ran to his sister's bed. She was flailing and screaming, drenched in sweat and her own blood.

Her brother gathered her up in his arms seeing that she was bleeding but unable to see from where. He shouted at the nuns that started to trickle in, demanding that they bring him bandages and rags. I stood there in horror and disbelief as I looked down at the chair beside her bed and saw Father Raphael's coat draped across the back.

Pulled from my thoughts, I heard Father Dulante rush past me. His fingers curled into my bicep and drug me to the bed where we began to try and hold her down. Miriam was pushing a long, round piece of wood into her mouth that resembled a bit that a horse would use, so she wouldn't swallow her tongue.

Louis was shouting to her as he rocked her trembling upper body while Father Dulante and I tried to hold her down. We were pleading with him to allow us to get to her upper body so that Miriam could find the source of her wound. I was worried that her wrists were reopened.

Louis gently lay Isabel back down on the bed and snatched the cloth from the closest nun, wiping his sister's face which looked as though it was covered with a red, leather mask. He was trying to swallow the sobs but his eyes welled with tears betraying him.

We all stared down at Isabel and the scent of jasmine rolled in thickly again. Her eyes rolled back into her head and she thrashed her head from side to side. Her hair was damp with her own blood and with each violent turn of her head, would splash those of us surrounding her.

Finally, suddenly, she stopped. She just lay there in a pool of blood and sweat, drifting off into a deep sleep where she panted and writhed like she was inflicted with fever. Miriam began to wipe her down and Louis covered his face with his hands, sobbing over his sister. It was only when Miriam gasped that he looked up again.

Isabel's feet were covered in blood and two perfect punctured holes bled slowly on the tops of her arches. I became weak in the knees and lowered myself to them, compelled to pray for this woman. Father Dulante made the sign of the cross and kissed his rosary before kneeling beside me to do the same.

Miriam turned in time to see Father Raphael enter. I felt him but I refused to let him deter me. The sound of the hissing and static whispers rose up louder and louder in my ears, threatening to steal my equilibrium but I held my ground. My voice was screaming in my own head as I prayed over it all.

The noise receded and Father Raphael stood behind Louis. I looked up as I finished my prayer in time to see the sadistic mask and slither of his long black tongue over his lips when his hand touched Louis' shoulder. I shouted and fell back, slamming my head against the chair behind me. I fought the darkness as it faded in to no avail. It finally won and I was unconscious.

When I awoke, I heard the sound of the birds in the distance and I kept my eyes closed a little bit longer hoping it was all a bad dream. Did angels dream? I didn't think so but I was in a human body and suffered human things.

Emotion was the biggest difficulty to tackle. I was thrown into this body like a newborn babe and I was flailing through everything. In the beginning, I had to learn what it meant to relieve myself. The pain in my stomach was so great until I felt the trickle of warm urine down my leg. It probably wouldn't have been so bad except my learning experience was sitting in a tavern asking the waitress what they ate "here".

She looked down at my feet toward the warm stream of urin, and started yelling obscenities at me, calling me a drunken idiot. I ran out into the night and staring down at my pants, which were too short on me, in disgust. An old woman who was passing, heard the commotion took pity on me, calling me to her. Wanting to be far away from the vulgar barmaid, I stumbled over to her, thankful for a distraction. My urine-drenched clothing clung to me, intensifying the briskness of the nocturnal breeze, but my escort seemed not to be bothered. She muttered something about the Devil's drink and began to preach to me as we walked to her home. I smiled, immediately warming up to her, letting her guide me to where she stayed. I sat up with her for most of the night sharing a kettle of stew and freshly baked bread. Her home was humble. There were holes in the roof and walls allowing for a terrible draft to enter, chilling her old body to the bone.

The Lord was a carpenter and my favorite lesson of his was how he would take rough, raw materials and make beautiful items from them. I decided that I would help this woman who took pity on me. Over the next seven weeks, I fixed up the shack and made it a home.

I fixed the stairs so that she did not catch her worn shoes on the nails and fall. I fixed the holes in her roof so that she did not get wet and suffer a cold from the dampness. I patched the holes in the walls so that the warmth from her fire would keep her comfortable during the winter months and cold nights.

It was the night before I was to set off on my task to find Isabel when old lady Anne died peacefully in her sleep. I felt her spirit tickle my cheek and I opened my eyes to stare up into her lovely face. The Lord was beside her and she knew me for what I was.

It was a morning with the same sounds as I heard now. The birds chirped in the distance and I felt fresh winds on my cheek as I lay under the open porch but somehow I knew I was not back there again with Anne. I opened my eyes and saw the Lord at my table, admiring a jug I carved from wood. Around the surface were intricate details of Heaven and he glanced up at me from them.

"This is beautiful. From one carpenter to another, I applaud your workmanship." He said, ever present smile on his face as bright as the morning.

"Thank you, my Lord." I was genuinely touched by his praise.

I sat up and walked over to where he was standing. He began to pour the water that was in the jug into two cups before motioning with his hand for me to sit down and talk with him. Without hesitation I did, quietly observing my greatest teacher as he moved.

When he sat down we were eye to eye and I never realized that before this moment. We were the same height in human form. My entire body relaxed and I felt at ease once more in his presence. Wrapping my hands around the cup he set before me, I took a drink of the water and knew that he touched it. It was cooler and purer than any water from the well I'd had before. Instantly it seemed to revive and refresh me. My smile let him know that I was aware.

"Sometimes, Marciel, we all need to have a moment to refresh our purpose and collect our thoughts." He said.

I listened to his words and nodded. I knew exactly what he meant. Even now I was collecting my thoughts as I spun the cup around between my hands, staring into that crystal clear water.

"When man was first created, we were jealous." I said, speaking of the angels. "Though, we did not know we were jealous because we had never felt mortal emotions as I do now." I looked up from the water into the Lord's eyes.

He smiled and remained silent but leaned back in his chair as a gesture that he was relaxed and wanting to hear what I had to say.

"I admire the humans now because it is so hard, Lord. It is so hard to have faith and follow God's plan when the plan is so obscure." I was past the tears and the fear now as I spoke. I was frustrated.

"Our Father in Heaven created all that you see here. The heavens and the earth. Could he be incapable of understanding his own creations?"

My brows furrowed and I felt suddenly ashamed. Letting out a sigh, I too, leaned back in my chair and shook my head. Something still felt wrong.

"No."

The Lord stood up and walked to the window, his cup still in his hand as he spoke leisurely. I watched as the sunlight moved just to caress his face. His flawless complexion glowed in that light which became a halo over his head when he turned to me again.

"Have not the saints suffered in the name of God?" He asked.

"Yes, they have." I replied.

"Have not they been rewarded in Heaven for their suffering here on earth?"

"Yes, Lord."

"Treasures and comfort of this earth are nothing. The humans know they must store their rewards and crowns in Heaven. It is far more important."

I offered him a small smile and nodded again. I knew that he sensed I was still not happy with the answer but he did not push. Walking to our table again, he sat down leaning forward onto his elbows to level his gaze at me.

"You're right, Marciel. It is not easy to be human." He said, then reached across that table to pat my hand. "Did you forget that I, too, was human for over thirty years? I went through birth and death and suffering as a human. I know what you feel."

Immediately, I felt the guilt. How could that have slipped my mind? Of course he knew what I felt. I looked up, meeting his gaze and felt my strength return but the sadness of my weakness increased.

"I am an unworthy servant, Lord. I will not question why you chose me; I will only have faith that whatever reason it was, I am the perfect choice for the task."

His smile grew and I felt my heart swell. It is impossible not to feel joy when your maker shows pride in you. He stood once more and walked to the window, dissolving in the light. I felt his absence as soon as he was gone.

It was then that I realized it was 7 am. The start of the boys' choir warm up had begun. I went to the basin at the side of my bed and washed up before hastily throwing on my clothes to check on Isabel.

ISABEL: BUT NOT TONIGHT

Isabel had, had the dream since she was a little girl. Each time it was the same scenario. Fire rain down from the Heavens, calls from a trumpet filled the skies, wings blocked out the sun, and screams filled the air. It was a message from God. She had no idea what it meant, or if it would happen in a literal sense but every night that she had the dream, she would wake up crying, and reaching out for something.

It was no different tonight.

Isabel jerked awake and found that this time she was clutching her abdomen. It was her thirteenth birthday today. Her nurse told her about things that happened to a girl's body when she turned this age. Swallowing hard, she slowly lifted the blankets to see if she had stained her linens. She could already feel the warm, moisture between her thighs. Her heart began to speed up, afraid to see the blood. No matter how prepared they tried to make her, she would never be prepared enough to wake up in her own blood.

Grimacing slightly, she took a deep breath. The cramps made her stomach feel like it was being pulled from the inside out. Panting softly, she doubled over when another cramp hit her as if she was being crushed by a raging bull. The moisture between her legs grew and she let out a slow groan. Throwing back the blankets, she looked down and began screaming.

In the pool of blood, a child was squirming. It let out a shrill cry, filling the room and piercing her ears. Covered in afterbirth, its slick skin writhed against hers, and Isabel shoved her heels deep into the bed, pushing herself away from it. The long umbilical cord unraveled but kept her tethered to the infant. Letting out another horrified scream, she felt the world tremble. Her body was being rocked violently and the more she screamed, the more her body shook until finally she could hear a voice in the distance calling her.

"Isabella!" It shouted, cutting through the screams.

Isabel stopped screaming long enough to look around and find her nurse.

"Mari, please! Help me!"

Mari's hand gripped Isabel from somewhere. Her voice was suddenly as clear as day, and no longer far away, "Isabella, wake up!"

Mari's voice was firm and demanding of Isabel's compliance. Isabel opened her eyes with a deep, gulping inhale. Mari was fending off Isabel's clawing and kicking limbs, while trying to curl the girl into the protective embrace of her arms.

"Isabella, it's all right! Shhh." Mari whispered against her ear, tightening her arms around the frantic young girl.

Isabel was gulping in more air between sobs. Drawing her knees to her chest, she piled her entire body into her nursemaid's lap. Mari rocked her gently, and hummed while running her fingers through the damp, matted curls of Isabel's hair. Working the knots out, she alternated hands. One wiped away the beads of sweat from her forehead, the other separating the twisted nest of hair caused by her thrashing.

"Look," she chided softly and playfully, "now we'll have to redo your hair for the party."

Isabel was still trembling but began the slow process of calming down. The longer she was awake, the further the dream faded away. Finally, opening her eyes, she looked down to her nightgown. It was dry and clean, except for the sweat from the exertion and fear.

“Do you wish to tell me about it?” Mari moved so that she could look into Isabel’s eyes.

Isabel shook her head. Talking about it would force her to remember. Remembering it would bring the images to her mind again. She couldn’t bear it. Maris nodded her head and brushed Isabel’s hair away from her eyes.

“Let’s get you cleaned up and put your new dress on. I’m sure your mother and father can’t wait to see you in it.”

Isabel forced a smile and sat up. The girls were sent in when Mari exited to assist her. Two of the girls were Isabel’s age, three were older. The eldest was Anna, who did Isabel’s hair. She loved the braids and twists that Anna adorned her with, and the gentle hand she used soothed Isabel to a calm state. Anna’s face was a welcome sight when she came through the door.

The second eldest was Sofie. She was the seamstress for Isabel and her mother. She made sure that all of Isabel and her mother’s clothing not only fit but lay impeccably without a thread out of place. Sofie’s soft voice came wafting in before she turned the corner and Isabel’s smile became less fake and more sincere.

The third eldest woman was in charge of Isabel's hygiene and jewelry. Handing Isabel a rag, and a bowl of watered spices as she approached, she would supervise while the young woman cleaned her teeth. The strong herbs stung momentarily at Isabel's lips and gums but she rubbed them in. Satisfied, the older woman named Beth handed her a cup of water to rinse.

When Isabel was done, Beth supervised the two girls who were of Isabel's age as they washed her hands and feet. One of the girls, Amy, used a small stick to get under her finger and toe nails. The other, Jane, began affixing her jewelry. Placing the rings on her fingers, Jane walked behind Isabel and placed the new strand of opals and rubies that her mother had commissioned for this occasion around her neck. The gold wrapped around her throat snugly and then a delicate chain cascaded downward, finished with a cross that was handset with matching rubies.

"You look so beautiful, Isabel." Amy announced, pulling her to the mirror to look for herself.

Isabel took in a soft breath at the sight of the beautiful piece, gingerly bringing her fingers up to trace the curl of the gold filigree. Sofie placed a few decorative flowers in her hair and they all giggled before stepping back and letting her look at her reflection.

The dress was white with embroidered, red roses all the way down to the hem. Her hair coiled in beautiful curls down her shoulders and tied back with a red sash. The splash of white flora against her dark strands made her eyes sparkle. The way the necklace cradled the base of her long, swan-like neck almost brought tears to Isabel's eyes. Glancing down, she saw that Sofie even managed to make her slippers match, perfectly.

Stepping into them, she laughed.

"All this fuss! Just for my birthd-" the words cut off from her throat as she looked up, and into the mirror, again.

In its reflection, she saw the ladies but their faces were disfigured and twisted into horrifying grins. The hollow of their eyes were blacked out. Their teeth gnashed and their jaws opened wide, allowing black tongues to whip and coil down past their chins.

Isabel screamed and looked to her neck. The red jewels were replaced with a slit in her throat that gaped angrily and bled down the front of her chest into the white satin of her dress. She choked and grasped at her neck trying to stop the bleeding, but the blood leaked and sprayed past her fingers and onto the stone floor. The girls swooped in like vultures. Their hands grabbed at her flesh and she looked on in terror as the mirror reflected the image of her body being torn to pieces.

"Isabel!" Amy cried and tried to pull her away from the mirror.

Isabel jerked away and spun, again. This time she knocked the tray over and the water with the herbs splattered all over the floor. Skittering away and back against the furthest wall, Isabel faced the ladies. Their reflection no longer in front of her, all five of them looked at her with concern and bewilderment. Afraid to reach out for her again, they stood there in stunned silence.

Mari ran in again and brushed past the girls, "Isabella? What is it!?"

Isabel's first reaction was to pull away but Mari got ahold of her and kept her still. Isabel's eyes filled with tears and she shook her head with confusion.

"What is happening to me?" She cried.

Mari's hands slowly collected Isabel until she was fully within her embrace. Isabel's knees gave in and she crumpled to a heap on the floor surrounded by the others.

“Go, Amy. Fetch something to clean the floor.” Mari ordered, shooing the girl with one hand while keeping the other around Isabel.

Amy remained still for a several breaths, staring at Isabel before she was able to process the movement from her brain to her feet. She returned just seconds later with the towels. Going to her knees, she mopped up the water but kept glancing over at Isabel. Sofie stood back, frowning as she mourned the efforts she put into the dress which was now in a crumpled, wrinkled pile on the floor with Isabel in the center.

“She saw something in the mirror.” Sofie said, pointing at it.

Maris looked over her shoulder at the mirror and the reflection. Nothing seemed amiss but Isabel continued to shy away and avert her eyes from it.

It took almost twenty minutes to calm Isabel down this time and convince her that she was probably suffering from the stress of her nightmare and the excitement of her party that evening. Mari persuaded her to look in the mirror, confirming that it was just her imagination. When she finally conceded and gazed into its reflection, Isabel’s brows furrowed. Her concern was growing into a full panic, now.

“I think we should call the doctor in. Maybe he will prescribe a tonic to calm your nerves.” Mari said, once more combing her fingers through Isabel’s hair.

“Please, don’t tell my mother and father, Mari. I don’t want them to worry. Let them enjoy the party. They worked so hard on it.” Isabel squeezed Mari’s hand as she pleaded with her.

Mari considered it for a bit then finally agreed, “All right but if anything else happens I will tell them, straight away.”

“Yes, nurse, I understand.” Grateful for Mari’s cooperation, Isabel moved to the bench in front of her vanity and waited the doctor’s visit.

The doctor came and did a brief physical examination then concocted the tonic for her which she drank, quickly. The strength of the medicine caused her to wince and make a face but she got it all down. Within minutes, she was drifting off to sleep on the soft fur blanket of her bed.

Mari sat beside Isabel on the chair that was beside her and began to knit while she waited for the girl’s nap to end. Every now and then, she’d pause and check on her. She smiled softly and leaned in, placing a kiss to side of her forehead. Mari had looked after Isabel since she was just a baby. This was a big day for her, but also for Mari and Isabel's parents. Today she would meet George. George was one of the suitors for Isabel's hand in marriage. Their parents would allow them to meet, then begin talks of negotiation for their betrothal if everything went as planned. Of the two that showed interest in Isabel, George is the one that Mari favored, the most.

Kneeling down beside Isabel's bedside, Mari pulled out her rosary. Pressing the crucifix against her lips, she kissed the well-worn metal and closed her eyes to pray for her girl. Not even the first word was whispered before the woman's eyes snapped open suddenly. She tried to take in a breath but the rosary was snaked around her neck and the beads dug into her skin.

Mari's fingers clutched at the rosary, trying to pull it from her throat. Tears were welling up in her eyes as she looked toward the mirror to see who or what was attacking her. She choked out a scream when she saw the reflection of a girl that looked like Isabel but Isabel was asleep in front of her! Coal-like eyes gazed back at the woman as she struggled to free herself from its grasp. Slowly the room was growing dim and Mari's consciousness began to slip before the beads snapped and hit the stone, followed by the sound of the bedroom door opening and a rush of skirts. The girls ran toward Mari to assist her, assaulting her with questions as to what happened.

Mari's vision returned and she rushed to her feet. Pushing past the ladies, the woman ran for the door, screaming. Isabel finally awoke to the commotion and caught sight of Mari as she left. The girls turned back to look at Isabel who slowly sat up, still in a drug induced haze.

Amy knelt down and picked up the crucifix along with some of the beads, holding them up in her hand, "What happened?"

Isabel and the other girls stared at the pieces of the rosary in her hand and shook their head in silence. Mari never returned, and Isabel was so heartbroken that she had a new rosary made with pieces of Mari's. From that day onward, she kept it with her at all times.

There were times when Isabel would ask her parents what happened, or if the two had ever heard from her, again. The two would exchange odd looks before changing the subject. It wasn't until Isabel was sixteen that she'd overheard one of the staff whispering to another that just three days after Mari ran from Isabel's room, she was found hanging from the rafters of her bedchambers.

Isabel sat on her heels, remembering it all. A year has passed since she'd entered into her service at the abbey. Rolling one of the beads of her rosary between her fingertips, she let out a sigh and closed her eyes. Mari was like a mother to her. Re-living the events was heart-wrenching for her. She was still kneeling before the cross in her room when she began to pray.

There was a sudden, loud banging on her door that snatched her out of her prayers instantaneously. Grabbing the hems of her skirts, she rushed toward the door.

"Who is it?" She whispered loudly.

There was no answer and Isabel's heart began to play catch up with her breathing. She backed away from the door and ran to the small table beside her bed to grab her candle. Before her fingers could lock around the handle of its base, the banging continued, again. Her spine locked and she grabbed the candle, spinning on a heel to face the door.

"Who—who is it!" she shouted and her voice cracked ever so slightly.

Still, there was no answer. The handle of the door jiggled and Isabel backed up. The noise stopped as sudden as it began, leaving the echoing silence that rang against her ears. Realizing that her jaw was open and hanging there, she closed it, admonishing herself.

"This is ridiculous, Isabel. Answer the d.."

The sound of the door being slammed against from the other side made her rush back to it. Frozen fingers twisted the knob and she threw open the door, expecting for someone to fall inside. A gust of wind followed the opening of the door, but there was nothing and no one there.

Taking a few cautious steps forward, Isabel peeked outside the threshold of the doorway and looked left, then right. Nothing. The entire hallway was empty. She found herself gripping the rosary between white knuckled fingers. Forcing her legs to move, she rushed to the door and slammed it shut. Shaky fingers fumbled with the lock before it slid into place. Once she heard it connect, she ran backwards, keeping her eyes fixed on the door. Her eyes never left it until she saw the glow of candle light grow larger against the wall where she had begun her prayers. The light and the heat grew more intense, forcing her to take her eyes from the door to see what the source of it was.

The small flame of the candle grew to a miniature pyre, reaching higher and higher. Her eyes followed it to the tip until she saw it illuminate the crucifix, again. Blood began to ooze from the wounds of Christ down her wall. Crawling on all fours, Isabel raced to find her rosary. As soon as her fingers got close to it, she was thrown back and pinned to the wall. She tried to cry out for help but something forced her lips shut. Tossing her head to the side, she curled her fingers and pulled at her mouth, trying to break free of her confinement. Her hair slithered up along her chin and began feeding its way into her skin, pushing deeper until it pierced through to the other side. Needling its path, it began to sew the girl's lips together.

Hours later, Isabel's mother found her lying there on the floor unconscious. Calling for help, she began lifting from under Isabel's arms to try and move her onto the bed. Her father was in the hallway with George's father when they heard the cry for help and ran in to assist her. Isabel's father, Louis, was furious. It was obvious to him that this was something that had been going on for a while but no one thought to let him know.

"What is wrong with her!" He yelled at his wife.

Undeterred by her husband's roar, Blanche barked at them to bring the girl to the bed. When they lowered her down, Blanche wrapped her in blankets and dismissed her husband's wrath. George's father,

John, stepped back while exchanging glances between the two. Sensing the watchful eye, Blanche pointed her gaze toward her husband and forced a smile.

"She is fine, Louis. Very excited for the evening, I believe. The girls have been running around all day getting ready." Motioning with her eyes quickly at the observer, she masked her anger at her husband's scene with a smile aimed at John.

"All she's talked about since this morning is meeting your son, and hoping that he is not disappointed."

It seemed to work.

John bowed graciously to Blanche, "It is my hope that he finds her to be more than he ever imagined."

Bowing again, he cut his gaze toward Louis, his frown softening to concern and empathy, "Allow me to take my leave so that you can tend to your daughter. I will see you this evening, yes?"

Louis gave a grateful nod of his head, "Thank you for your assistance, John. Yes, tonight. It shall be a celebration for both our families."

The families parted ways and half past the hour, Isabel finally awakened. The girls pounced into action, bustling so chaotically they ran into one another more than once. Isabel tried to sit up but her head began to swim. Her mother reached out to her, holding a cup of water.

"Drink, girl. We need to get you up and ready for the celebration."

Groaning softly, Isabel took the cup obediently. Taking a sip, she let out a soft, relieved sigh and eased her way out of bed. Within an hour, she was dressed and ready. The girls laughed softly as they surrounded her until her mother chided them.

"Tch! We are ladies, not a gaggle of swallows. You are to walk with immaculate posture, keep your eyes down and chin up."

To punctuate her commands, she slid her hand toward one of the girls and placed the tip of her fan beneath her chin, giving it a slap. The girl choked back a gasp and went rigid at the spine. Blanche's face twisted into a cold smile of satisfaction and she turned, opening the door for them to make their way into the ballroom.

There was a soft swishing of satin hems over the thick, cowhide carpets as the procession came into view. The audience who waited expectantly paused and let out a quiet rush of "ohh's" and "ahh's". One by one, the girls entered to their announced names until finally it was the Queen's turn. From the corner of her mouth, she whispered harshly to Isabel.

"Do not make a fool of me, girl. I've worked too hard for this."

Then just as instantly as the horns began, the Blanche of Castile turned her head and smiled gracefully, then made her grand entrance, walking past the court until she arrived beside her King. Taking her seat, she nodded to the man near the door and he began the announcement for Isabel.

Isabel stepped forward and did everything her mother asked her to. She was a shining gem among all who attended. None could take their eyes off her, including her intended, George, who greeted her at the end of the carpeted aisle. The two exchanged bows and he offered her his hand, which she took graciously. Escorting her to center of the dance floor, the two waited for the music to start then began their waltz. It was the first night in forever that Isabel felt normal. She laughed her worries away and danced into the late hours of the night.

Working up a hunger, she placed her hand upon George's shoulder, "Please, M'Lord. Might take my leave to eat?"

George, already entranced by his intended, bowed and placed a kiss upon the back of her hand, "I could never deny you anything, M'Lady."

Isabel's eyes were dreamy as she gazed into his, but hunger won the battle and she finally pried herself from his company to settle down at a table. The wine seemed to flow like a fountain, never-ending. She and the other guests drank their fill and ate until corsets pinched at the figures of the ladies wearing them. Isabel was pulled in every direction to dance and play among her guests until she realized that she had not seen George for some time. Laughing freely at the silliness of the court's royal cast as they performed, she searched the sea of faces for her betrothed. Not finding him, she grew somewhat concerned and made her way toward the dark hallways outside the ballroom. The staff brushed past her quickly, trying to keep up with the demand for food and drink, muttering apologies while balancing dishes and platters. Isabel smiled and dismissed them to their work as she continued her search.

There was a noise at the end of the hallway, in the shadows and she frowned but walked toward it. She heard rustling and thought perhaps one of the guests got lost or drunk and could not find their way through the maze of corridors. The music and laughter faded into the distance and Isabel walked slowly forward, her racing heart warning her of what she may discover.

More rustling and a woman's groan made Isabel pause. She listened intently and heard the whispers of a man and woman engaged in a lover's whisper. Not knowing what prompted her forward, Isabel moved forward suddenly and rounded the corner but was stopped short by the display before her.

George had his hand up one of her ladies' skirts, and her legs were entwined around his waist. Her exposed breasts were mashed into his face while he grunted and pressed into her like a starved animal. Each thrust knocked the girl's spine into the wall behind her and she was lost to the act until her half-closed eyes found focus on Isabel's stunned face. The embarrassed girl began to slap George's shoulder, each one a little rougher until he stopped.

"What, girl?! Don't be coy, now!" His smile faded when he saw the look of fear on her face, her hands desperately trying to cover herself.

George twisted to see who had caught them in the midst of their stolen moment, only to be taken aback by the revelation that it was his intended wife.

Whispers filled Isabel's head like a thousand beating, leather wings. Her breath came short and fast, causing her chest to rise and fall rapidly. They were saying something and reaching out for her but it rose from her belly. Her hand rose, finger pointed at the couple who were now in a state of panic. Isabel tried to fight it but could not restrain the horrible growl that tore at her vocal chords, overflowing into screaming condemnation.

"Whore!" the shout echoed off the corridor's walls, stopping the music with the residual clinking of forks and glasses until everyone stopped.

Silence only fueled her tirade, consuming her with wrath as she stalked toward the girl striking her against her cheek, "Harlot!!"

George stumbled back, watching Isabel unleash fury on the girl who would not fight back. Slap after slap was followed now by closed fists that pummeled the girls face and head, "Devil's Whore!"

The girl tried to fend the blows off with her hands while forgetting that her dress left her completely exposed. The crowd had started to rush in to see what was going on only to be stopped by the scene ensuing before their witnessing eyes. Isabel had begun grabbing fistfuls of hair, jerking and yanking them off the helpless girl's bloody scalp.

The King forced his way through the awe-struck crowd and stumbled to a stop to the gruesome scene.

"Isabel!" He shouted.

His voice was lost to deaf ears, filled with the rushing of blood and the fire of her anger.

"Isabel!!" He shouted louder this time and grabbed his daughter, pinning her arms to her sides so that they could deal no more blows.

Isabel screeched like an animal and thrashed until all energy was spent, then went limp, sobbing in her father's arms. Her father was filled with his daughter's anguish and shame to which he dealt to the cowering couple.

"You bring shame upon my house!?" Words spit from between his lips and he spun Isabel toward her mother who was finally able to get beside her husband.

Catching her daughter, she tried to comfort her but peered dangerously over her head at the two who had ruined the night but most importantly, her plans for setting up her empire of power.

"George!" The voice came from his father this time.

John stood there, towering over the rest of the men in all his intimidating stature. The men moved quickly from the man's path, allowing him through. A large hand swung across his leather bound chest, striking his son with such force, the boy crumpled to the floor.

It wasn't until the sun was peeking over the horizon by the time the effects of the night began to wear off. Isabel's lady was hauled off to who knows where, George was carried by the nape of his neck by his father who offered every apology he could to the King and Queen, and Isabel was carried upstairs to her room. In a rare show of kindness, her mother bathed her and consoled her, washing the blood and bits of scalp from her fingernails.

Isabel could only stare off into the distance between uncontrollable fits of sobbing. Curled up in her mother's arms and dressed in fresh linen, Isabel drifted off into a deep sleep.

When consciousness left her, she became aware of a light shining in the distance. She was in a lucid dream and unable to move her limbs. She felt her body grow weightless and her spirit freeing from the shell of herself until she turned and was able to look upon her own sleeping form, nestled beside her mother. Blanche was drifting off, her head bobbing in steady rhythm as she fought against torpidity.

A voice called to Isabel, beckoning her to follow it. She moved slowly in this form but followed the compulsion to pursue. The curtains that covered the windows blew gently, giving hint to a bright red light from behind the thick material. With a slow, steady stride, she continued to move toward them, reaching her hand out. *It was taking so long!* She thought. Determination furrowed her brow and she focused, each step growing more coordinated and faster. When she reached the curtains, which were only a few feet from where her body lay, it seemed like hours had passed and she had exerted all of her strength. Lethargy was beginning to take over, but she did not give in.

She realized then, that she felt heat coming from behind the drapes, and her fear rose like a powerful wave. Forcing her limbs to move, she gripped the corner of the material throwing it back. A burst of heat and flames shattered the thin glass embedding the shards within her eyes and face. Trying to shield herself from the explosion, she struggled to make sense of it all. *How can I feel this?!*

Without further warning, something gripped her and she opened her eyes against the stinging pain, the heat of the fire and the veil of blood hindered her sight but she saw the face of a beast moving in. Isabel screamed and tearing at its face with her nails, digging at the hard flesh until something more hideous was revealed. She continued to throw her fists at it but was rendered paralyzed again. The blackness surrounded her, filling her lungs like the waters of a dark ocean. She could not scream, or cry for help. She was drowning!

Kicking and flailing as hard as she could, she came to the surface of the water with a deep, drag of air into her lungs, forcing the dreams back to their world and her into reality. Her mother was screaming and her father was trying to restrain her. Isabel was consumed by the confusion and pushed to make sense of it all. Her eyes rolled around until they took in the sight of her mother's face. *What happened to her!?*

Scratches cut deeply into her mother's cheek and neck. The ladies were trying to press bandages and towels to them but Blanche was in hysterics, fighting them off of her.

"Get the girl out of my sight!" her mother howled.

Isabel could not control her own motor functions. She could feel her eyes rolling back into her head, then down again. Her fingers and toes contorted, painfully, and she began to froth at the mouth. Her entire body was rigid, forcing her spine to twist and her head to cock to the side. She was frozen this way for hours.

The next day, her father brought in the Holy See. He wanted a guarantee of his daughter's soul, and to be convinced she was not touched by evil.

Isabel was once again bathed and re-dressed before being brought into private consul with the head of the Catholic Church. They spoke at length, dined together, and prayed with one another before finally emerging that evening.

The King stood there in his chambers, waiting for the Priest to come with word. When he did, Louis was relieved to know that she was in fact suffering from the Passion; A divine gift from God himself, a calling to do his work.

"Isabel has been called to join the nunnery." The Priest dipped his jewel-adorned fingers into the bowl of fruit that was set upon Louis' table.

The King sat in silence for so long that his Grace continued on, "You have a son and a fierce wife, Louis. There is no need to fear for your crown."

The fat, purple grape was tossed between stained teeth, the dark skin visible as he continued to speak, spitting pieces of its juicy flesh as he did, "This is good for your cause. I give it my blessings."

With a wipe of his hand, the grape juice smeared the otherwise perfectly white silk. The priest seemed to give it no mind as he held his hand out, exposing the royal signet that squeezed circulation from the male's knuckle.

Louis swallowed back a small gag before pressing a barely-there kiss of his lips across the edge of it, hoping not to get anything in his mouth.

"I have a trusted friend that can take her into the abbey for training. Give me your permission to take her and she will head there with me on my way back to Rome."

The King watched the priest's chin waggle as he spoke before turning away and gazing into the fireplace. The heat caused small beads of perspiration to pool on his features and he wiped them away with his hand before nodding, in silence, giving his consent.

THE DARKNESS: AN INTERLUDE - LUCIFER

Father Raphael stood in front of the giant mirror. The surface was black and inky, swirling like oil. The tendrils of smoke slowly reached out for him like long spindly fingers to caress his chiseled form. He closed his eyes and allowed the touch before gazing deep within the dark abyss again. He would watch the humans from here, along with his minions whom he put into place to guide and manipulate Isabel's path until he had her just where he wanted her.

A pious and chaste girl, he saw the favor she held with The Father. Her beauty moved him and provoked the already festering and boiling jealousy buried within his blackened soul. His eyes narrowed as he watched her, peeling away her clothing with his lecherous stare. She aroused in him a desire he'd never known before; the desire to *mate.*

Taking in a slow breath, he pulled the air into his lungs and held it there, absorbing the scents for miles around. Tipping back his head, he allowed the lids of his eyes to fall again. From each scent he knew exactly to whom or what it belonged. Images of what he inhaled appeared on the mirror's surface before him; except *one*.

With a flick of his eyes toward the ceiling, Raphael's senses went into high alert. Since the dawn of time he would catch whiffs of this scent but never could he place or to whom it belonged. Adding to the danger, the mirror reflected nothing – a Void.

With a growl, he turned and raced toward it, eager to hunt this presence down and to know, once and for all, who or what its owner looked like. Pushing past the faces of mortals who never saw him due to the speed at which he traveled. They seemed to stand there, unmoving, as he maneuvered through their lifeless bodies. Animals were a different story – they sensed him but could not see him, unless he willed them to. This sometimes spooked the beasts and caused them to jerk, or bolt, suddenly.

He came to the river and skimmed across the surface on his belly like a serpent, zigzagging across the motionless ripples before diving under then pushing his speed again until he reached the bank. Springing out of the water like the jaws of an alligator, he landed in a crouch, low to the earth. He kept his eyes upward but brought his nose downward to get a better catch of the scent within the damp soil. The world was unnaturally silent all at once. He caught a glimpse of movement outside of his peripheral, then growled. *What was this ... Thing?*

He'd been there with the Father for every birth of every creation. Neither one of them understood the origin of the presence he was attempting to track now. Nostrils flared and he relaxed his muscles when the Old Man stepped out from behind him, out from the thin line of trees that lead back to the monastery.

"It's here." Raphael said gruffly. "The Void."

The Old Man only nodded, then leaned forward on his walking stick and rested his chin upon wrinkled, old hands.

"I had it." Raphael's words seemed less confident as he spoke the words over his shoulder.

"No you didn't." Kind but stern eyes looked up at the Dark Man – his First Creation.

Within the older man's eyes, which were crystal blue like frozen ice just above the water, was a light so brilliant that Raphael was forced to turn his eyes down in respect, whether he wanted to or not.

"I will find it." He snarled, then turned to race back to his lair beyond the trees.

After a moment, the Old Man let out a steady sigh, "No, you won't." Then he lowered his walking stick into the earth and let the trees embrace him until he disappeared, but not before his ominous prediction was uttered into the wind, "It will find *Us*."

BLASPHEMOUS RUMORS - MARCIEL

I waved to Father Dulante as I passed the large, open double doors to their room. He reciprocated with a smile and nod, never skipping a beat as his hands led the boys in their scales. The sound was the closest thing to Heaven I had left some days, and it filled each corridor I walked through until I ascended the stairs to the top floor where Isabel's room was.

I saw that her door was slightly ajar and that familiar fear crept along my neck. Was Father Raphael going to be there? I approached the door and stretched out my hand, slowly opening the large door.

A soft haze of light fell down through the windows. The curtains were open and I saw Louis there beside Isabel's bed, reading from scripture to his sister who was sleeping in her bed. I could not help but smile. Standing there for a moment I let that scene play for a moment before I looked down at Isabel's wrists and feet.

She was bound again. Her wrists were bandaged but small spots of blood seeped through. She had fresh linen and clothes and her feet were bare except for the bandages around those wounds which had also seeped during the night.

Just as I frowned, Louis' voice called to me. "She's going to be alright." He said.

"Of course she is." I said before I stood looked at him, again.

Standing off the wall, I smiled and walked over to him. I looked toward the door again then back at Louis who was following my gaze. I could feel the same uneasiness in him that I felt.

"You feel it, too, don't you?" he asked.

"Feel what?" I asked but I already knew.

"There is something about that priest." He whispered, glancing every so often to the doorway.

I could only nod at first, too stunned that I was not the only one that felt the evil that Father Raphael gave off. Even now as we spoke, I could feel the chill rise on my neck along with the fine hairs.

"I must stay here beside her." He said. "If I don't, I fear something will happen to her. I just feel it."

"I'll help you." I said.

Louis looked up at me and a face of relief covered his features. He seemed to breathe then as if he was unable to before. He even looked older overnight. Sleep deprived eyes were blood shot and I knew he had been awake all night, keeping vigil over her.

"In my travels, and on the battlefield, I have seen many, many evils" he said, gazing from Isabel back up to me, "but never, have I felt fear and death as certain as I do, here."

I had to try and ease his fear and pain, even though I knew what he felt was real and true, "No, my Lord. She will be fine. Just as before." I stepped toward him, hopeful that I was able to mask my emotions well enough to actually lie.

Louis tried to smile but it was only to hold back the tears. Isabel lie in a deep, fitful sleep beside him. He took her hand within his own and brought it to his lips before letting the tears break and fall down his cheeks.

I tore my gaze away from him, respectfully and looked toward his companion Felipe. The man's jaw tightened seeing his friend and sovereign reduced to such emotion. We both felt helpless. In battle, there was action and metal and swords. There was a result. In this moment, there was nothing we could do but stand and watch.

"Has she spoken at all?" I finally asked.

Louis shook his head, softly. "She speaks but it is nothing I can decipher. Languages I have not ever heard."

My eyes snapped quickly over at Felipe to this revelation. He nodded his head to confirm before turning back toward the window. His eyes fixed on something in the distance that piqued my curiosity. Standing slowly, I pressed my hand to Louis' shoulder and offered what comfort I could.

"Pray, my Lord. God will give us the strength we need to rise in victory."

Louis closed his eyes and let out a long, slow breath and lifted his bible again but nearly dropped it. He was exhausted. Gently, I took it from his grasp and spoke, lifting him with a guiding hand toward the door.

"There is a room set up for you next door, my Lord. Go wash up and take a nap. I will not leave her side even for a moment." I said.

Louis seemed torn and I squeezed his shoulder, reassuringly, nodding that it was okay. He appeared to give in, then. He knew that he could not stay awake much longer and accepted that he needed help. His companion stayed up with him guarding the door and I looked over at him, too.

"You go with your Lord and clean up. Take a nap and come back when you have had sufficient rest."

The man looked over at Louis and Louis nodded, dismissing him from his post. Hesitantly, the companion gave a small bow then turned to go. Louis leaned forward and kissed his sister's brow before turning to me once more.

"It's alright" I said, "Father Dulante will be up after boys' choir to look in on her as well. We will both be here to sit with her."

That seemed to make it all the more convincing for Louis and he offered a weak smile. He knew Father Dulante would protect his sister with his life, just as he did long ago. He gathered some of his things and lifted up his bible before pausing. Staring down at it, the tears welled in his eyes and his jaw clenched to keep them from shedding, yet again. He set the bible on her bed beside her and took a deep breath before turning to leave.

"Thank you" he said to me. His voice was soft and humble as he added, "I'll be back very shortly."

"No thanks are necessary." I said, smiling up at him.

Louis exited and I waited a moment before I took a small vial from my pouch. It was the water that the Lord had served me in my room this morning. Watching the door, I dabbed a few drops on Isabel's forehead and around her bed before I sat beside her and very gently pressed the remaining drops to her lips.

As soon as the water hit her tongue she opened her eyes and smiled weakly. A soft sigh escaped her lips, then she closed her eyes again for a moment. Talking was a task for her in this state as she began to collect her thoughts.

"I needed that." She finally mustered up, "I was so thirsty."

I smiled down at her and brushed the hair from her face. Even now she was so beautiful. Her eyes were dark but her skin still held its natural glow. I remember thinking that she was much like the Madonna with her head tilted to the side the way it was right now.

I was about to speak when the presence of Father Raphael was felt again. I turned to look at the door and came face to face with the priest. My stomach felt ill like I would lose my bowels at any moment and my features deepened into a look of anger. Creatures such as myself cannot stand evil even in human form.

Father Raphael stared up into my eyes and smiled but it was not a natural smile; it never reached his eyes. It was plastered there coldly on his face before he turned her gaze down to Isabel.

“Good morning, Isabel. It’s good to see you’re awake.” He said.

I was staring sternly at Father Raphael and started to move between him and Isabel when Isabel suddenly hissed and growled. The sound was feral and foreign coming from her. When I turned to look at her, her eyes were narrowed and she was clenching her teeth at him.

I moved to try calming her down, shoving past Father Raphael. Just as I reached for Isabel, she ripped one of the binds from the leather strap and smashed me in the side of the head with Louis’ bible.

The blow was so strong that I stumbled and fell into the end table beside her, knocking the bowl of water over. Shaking my head I stared at Isabel who was spitting out obscenities at the priest while making vulgar motions with her hands.

I was completely stunned but Father Raphael did not seem surprised at all. He just stood there watching her as she writhed on the bed. Her hand was reaching for her skirts and lifting them up along her legs until she exposed herself to the priest.

I thrust myself at Isabel again, pinning her beneath me and pulling her skirts down as much as I could. She only laughed and craned her head around the side of mine to continue her obscene verbal lashing at Father Raphael.

"Why do you touch the little boys, Father?!" she yelled. "Are you afraid to fuck a woman?" she cackled and began to undulate beneath me.

I was flush with embarrassment but I continued to pin her arm down and retie the straps that kept her down. Once I had her retied she lunged toward me and tried to take a bite out of my cheek. I felt the graze of her teeth along my skin but moved just in time.

I fell back on the floor beside her bed in shock and my eyes were wide with fear as I stared at this horrible transformation of such a gentle woman. Father Raphael's steps were heard as he came around the side of Isabel's bed into my peripheral vision.

"I want her restrained. She's suffering from dementia." He said plainly.

The two nuns that always accompanied Father Raphael nodded and turned mechanically to comply. I could not move, I was completely frozen where I sat. This could not be happening.

Father Raphael turned his head slowly to gaze down at me before he slid his fingers gently along Isabel's cheek. In horror I watched as she nuzzled his fingers and laughed at me.

He stepped back and the two nuns returned with a leather mask and shackles. I stood up to protest but felt hands along my arms pulling me back. Two unknown, older priests were restraining me as well!

Isabel was retied and the new shackles put in place before they began to place the mask over her eyes. She let out a horrible scream that made my whole spine seem to melt. Even the boys' choir stopped. Her scream left the monastery silent for only a few seconds but those few seconds felt like eternity before I heard Louis' shouts.

He appeared at the door and lunged for Father Raphael. The priest slammed against the wall and growled at Isabel's brother before shoving him back into the crowd of priests that now began to filter in. The men held Louis back as the two exchanged words.

"Are you mad?!" Father Raphael growled.

"You will not get away with this!" Louis shouted as he pulled himself from the grasp of the priests.

"This is a church matter, Louis. Surely, you do not wish me to have you removed." The priest hissed at him.

Louis threw the men off him again and his companion burst through the door to assist him with sword drawn. Louis raised a hand to still him, knowing Father Raphael's pull with the Pope.

"It's alright Felipe. We are gentlemen and shall handle this with civility." Louis said.

It was a long, tense moment before Father Raphael finally dismissed the other priests. The ones behind me released me from their grasp and I turned to watch them go. Louis and Felipe were still tense and Felipe's hand was still resting on the hilt of his weapon when Father Raphael grinned at the three of us casually walking toward the door and exiting. His whistle echoed through the hallways.

Isabel was still being restrained as the priests began escorting Louis and his companion back to their room. He continued to struggle with them, pushing them off as he shouted, "I'm not leaving her side!"

The two nuns that were restraining Isabel sneered and shouted back at him, "We must clean her and redress her wounds. You cannot be in here!"

Louis was not hearing any of it, until Miriam came rushing through them all. "What is it? What has happened?"

The steam left Louis' fight slightly when she showed up, his hand extended toward his sister, "She has gone into fits of rage again." He turned and paced toward the hallway before trying to rush through the crowd of priests who quickly deterred him, once again. Louis let out a growl and Felipe was growing restless to use his sword, but waited like a patient and faithful comrade for the command.

Miriam's hand reached out for Louis' placing it within her own, "I'll stay with her. It's OK. I'll stay and watch her." She waited for his eyes to rest on hers before she continued her reassurance. "I will make sure she is tended to, my Lord."

Louis was still pressing against the barricade of robes but slowly backing down. I stood there in the doorway, ready to assist him should he choose to wage war on the cluster of strange priests who seemed to come from nowhere. I'd never seen their faces before that day. Louis backed away slowly, keeping his deathly gaze upon the robed man in front of him in silent warning. Felipe and I followed his lead, and I gave Miriam a backward glance as we made our way back into the hallway, letting her know that should she need us, we would be there.

Louis paced down the hallway, wearing a path in the stone. Exhaustion was eating away at his patience and his wit. Each time we tried to get him to rest, he would be roused from it to rush to Isabel's side again. I realized then, it was intentional. He was being worn down, on purpose. Getting him to rest now would be nearly impossible. The truth was, they were all tired and being worn down. I had to finally admit that I was part of that group, too.

It felt like hours, though it was only 30 minutes, before the door to Isabel's room opened. The twin nuns exited and paused. Eerily, they moved in sync with one another as if they shared one mind, and one thought. The two glanced back at our small group and I could see their eyes for a brief glimpse were not human. They wanted me aware. Knowing that I was, they smiled and turned back toward the opposite direction, continuing down the hall.

I stood up a little too quickly, drawing the attention of Louis and Felipe and rushed toward Isabel's room. The two felt the urgency and followed quickly behind. Father Dulante came around the corner just as I reached the doorway and saw the look of concern on our drawn faces before he, too, rushed over.

"What is it, Marciel?" He whispered, quietly. "Is she alright?"

His eyes dropped from mine to the door where my hand was, waiting with anticipation for me to open it so that he could see for himself the answer to his question. I did not make him wait. I turned the knob and entered cautiously and without making hardly any noise in case she was asleep. It was important, now more than ever, that we all rested as much as possible.

Isabel was lying peacefully in bed with clean clothing and dressings. I started to smile as I continued inward but it melted away when I saw Miriam lying on the floor. Louis rushed past me to Isabel's side, protectively but kept his eyes on the fallen sister. I went down beside her and grabbed her hand, the warmth was a welcome to my fears. Father Dulante was torn on where to go first, but seeing Louis had Isabel, he rushed to Miriam's side and pressed his fingers to her neck, feeling for a pulse.

"It's weak but she's alive." He said, frowning more deeply as he made further assessment of her condition. Felipe whispered something under his breath and stood by the door. His hand reached for something on his belt and I could see it was a small book attached to a chain. He wore a miniature bible, and I thought how brilliant that was..and how like us angels, he seemed.

Father Dulante spoke up again, "Let's get her to a chair and off the floor. Ready?"

He waited until I nodded and we lifted her up and sat her down. Father Dulante held her head in his hands and patted her cheek as he looked at her closely, hoping to see her eyes open.

“Miriam?” He looked so determined and frightened. His hand pat her cheek a little more firmly, “Miriam!”

His shouts finally roused her and she wobbled her head slightly before her eyes opened and she gasped, pushing against the chair like she’d just come out of a nightmare. Father Dulante held onto her firmly and I clutched her hand again.

“It’s alright, Miriam.” I said, “We’re right here. It’s alright!”

It took her a moment to get her bearings and to focus on us before she finally calmed down and broke into sobs. I released her hand only to snatch a clean towel off the table in order to gently dab it at her lip which was split and bruised to a deep crimson purplish color. It had swollen to nearly double its size and looked extremely painful. She confirmed this by flinching at the slightest touch.

“Who did this to you!” Louis finally barked out.

Miriam looked at him with fearful eyes and glanced at Isabel. Even the suggestion made Louis’ face twist into fear and confusion. Isabel was lying there as if she’d not moved in days. His knees were weakened and he slowly went into a chair beside her, staring at her.

"I don't understand." He said. "How?"

He turned his gaze back onto Miriam. The fear and frustration blended away into guilt as he looked upon her injuries again. He turned to me, then Father Dulante who'd he'd known most of his life and pleaded for understanding.

"What is happening, Marco?"

Father Dulante shook his head silently. He had no words to offer. None that would ease any of Louis' worry. Ashamed of his helplessness, he turned and tried to find redemption by tending to Miriam's injuries. Handing him the rag, I stood and moved toward Isabel's side to check on her. Though she lie so still, her eyes moved rapidly behind her lids which had now begun to sink in from lack of sleep and nourishment.

"We must find a way to get your sister to eat, my Lord." I sat in the other chair, opposite of him trying to figure out when we'd be able to accomplish that between her violent outbursts and her lapsing into a deep, nightmare-filled sleep.

Time was slow and dreadful that day. Shadows grew longer along the wall and the sunlight gave in to the inevitable dusk. The three of us moved about like ghosts, barely speaking a word as we took turns tending to Isabel and trying to capture a few light naps in between shifts. Finally, as night approached, I resolved to pressing issue that lingered in my thoughts. I still needed to write. I needed privacy to do it, though. I gave out a light sigh and stood, facing them.

"My Lord, I beg your permission to take my leave for a while? I have some duties to tend to, and I'd like to clean up some."

Louis looked up and struggled with the decision. I could feel his hesitancy to relieve me, but he nodded. "Granted."

I gave a slight bow and turned to leave when he called after me, "Marciel, please return quickly. And be safe."

I offered another bow, "Yes, my Lord."

Straightening up again, I saw that his eyes never left Isabel and I nodded to the other three who stood rigidly. I knew the fear. Splitting up was not a favorable plan at the moment, but I had a duty to God, and to Isabel to commit everything to word and parchment.

I went to the door and opened it, then slipped out into the dark hallway on my way back to my chambers. After a few steps I realized that it had grown unusually cold and my flesh began to crawl with chill. Tucking my hands further into the bell of my sleeves, I quickened my pace and hurried on my way before I began to hear something, or someone, following me. Turning my head over my shoulder, I could not see more than a few inches from my face. Every torch was burnt out leaving me to find my way along the cold, black shadows that suddenly felt alive.

The crawling sensation I felt was no longer just the chill but something among the darkness that encompassed me. I jerked away, only to fall into the wall. To the left of me, something whispered my name and its cold breath washed over my ear. I lurched forward and fell to the ground scraping my knees as I crawled further away from whatever was there. I had no sense of direction, I just kept going before I suddenly ran into a pair of legs.

My shaky hands felt around for shoes or feet, but there were none. What I felt were hooves! At the single touch of fur at my fingertips, I cried out and flew back, again. It was madness! I was tossing myself back and forth against the walls from one point of danger to the next.

"Who is there?" I yelled out. In the back of my mind I hoped that someone would hear me and open their door or come rushing this way. I had nothing of the angelic soldiering I once had left within me, I had discovered. I was a trembling wreck.

No, I was wrong. I had one last weapon. Gripping my rosary in my grasp, I shoved it out toward the dark and shouted, "Oh Divine Father, Eternal Father in Heaven, in union with your Divine Son and Holy Spirit, I beg you to destroy your enemies beneath the might of your hand!"

A flash of light filled the hallway and blinded me before the concussion of its explosion threw me to yet another wall. The short glimpse I had of what was around me was horrific. Demons of every kind screeched as they were repelled by the light, and sent skittering and scratching against the stone back to the solace of the dark. In the absence of the light once more, the darkness was more potent. My eyes were still adjusting and I was trying to regain my footing when my throat was constricted within the grasp of an overpowering hand.

I tried to scream out. The sudden pressure of weight pushed the air from my lungs. I was struggling to breathe and to move away from the attack until I heard Father Raphael's voice in my ear. I could feel his teeth press against my skin as he spoke, searing my skin with his touch.

His saliva was like acid, blistering my skin causing me to choke out small cries of pain.

"You weak, pathetic, bag of flesh. Do you think can save them? Save *Her*? She is *mine* now. Our Father cannot save her, and nor can you. If you try, I will slay you, and the rest like lambs to the slaughter."

I fumbled for the rosary again, but he pushed harder. I could smell the sulfur on his breath, burning my lungs with what little oxygen was allowed within them. I could not see him. I could only writhe and struggle, blindly. He laughed before slamming my head into the stone behind it.

"They will suffer greatly, Marciel. Your weakness is growing. Your wings are gone. Your sword is gone. You are *nothing*. He has forsaken you, too. And you will die for him like the rest."

His words stung, emblazing the doubt on my heart and my soul. He was right. I was just a man. I was no match for Lucifer. Once my brother, now set out to destroy me, I could do nothing as he released his grip on my throat but crumple at his feet.

“Take him to his room and lock him in. He does not eat or drink without my permission.” Father Raphael’s command reached into the darkness.

The priest pivoted on a heel and stormed off into the shadows, leaving me to the hands of the priests that had restrained Louis earlier. The robed men grabbed me, their features concealed by the low, oversized cowls, and drug me to my chambers. The door slammed shut and I could hear the bolt slide into place, locking me inside.

For at least an hour I stayed there on my knees praying. I heard no voice from God. I had no visit from the Lord. I was alone. Whatever strength I did have, I used it to stand and faced my meager writing desk. The doubt that Lucifer had instilled in me was growing like a virus. I had to fend it off. I took steps toward the desk and felt sick.

“Oh God, help me!”

I let me head fall into my hands and wept. Not just for myself but for those that would die because I would fight for Isabel. Having shed enough tears, I lift my head and pushed past doubt to tend to my duty.

I AM YOU - MARCIEL

My quill rested against the papyrus and I took in a deep breath, letting it out slowly to clear my thoughts and mind before I began to document the events. I decided to begin with the family history of Isabel. As the words were etched into the parchment, the syllables were whispered around me and lifted into the air toward Heaven. I used angelic script so that no mortal could happen upon the book and read the sacred text. My fingers would arc each beautiful scripted letter in my very own hand.

Where it was necessary, I would also sketch out scenes on one or two pages. The face of Isabel was there now, staring back at me. Charcoal stained finger gently brushed the shading along her chin and high cheek bones as I reminisced at how beautiful she once was when I had first laid eyes upon her. The transformation happened so fast. She was already so petite that any slight variation in her weight showed more pronounced in her small heart shaped face. Even her hair, once shiny and healthy was ratted and clumped against her scalp. Forcing back the tears I continued my documentation of the past week in as much detail as he could.

Isabel Agustus born unto noble blood to Blanca Alphonsa, Queen of France and King Louis VIII, son and successor of Philip II (Philip Agustus) in the year of our Lord, twelve hundred and twenty five.

I stopped and stared at the words as I wrote them. My hand was possessed with its own life, documenting the events that I had gone through. My words would become permanent scripture in the Great Book and this was an honor that was reserved for only God's few chosen. As much as I wanted to smile with the accomplishment, I was brought down again that I could feel any such joy when Isabel was suffering – and suffering now – as I sat here.

With all the events that had transpired documented, I stood up and replaced the book into its hiding spot then pushed the bed back against the wall. I faced my room once more and decided that I would clean it. Cleaning it would help me sort through some things and organize my thoughts.

I picked up the plates and dumped the rotting food then used an old rag to clean off what little furniture I had left. I went to my desk and started to set the papers in a neat stack when there was a knock at my door. A smile came to my face as I recognized the soft rapping as Father Dulante's.

There was a small jingling of keys and then the sound of the lock being opened. When I opened the door, I saw him standing there with a small candle in his hand and a basket of what I assumed was food from the delicious smell. A knowing smile crossed my lips and I opened the door a little more to let him in.

"You deviant" I whispered, "disobeying Father Raphael and sneaking me food *and* breaking me out of my prison?"

Father Dulante laughed at my accusation then set the basket of bread and cheeses on the table before setting a carafe of wine down beside it. I handed him a clean cloth to wash his hands. Pulling out a chair, I sat down across from him and took the bread graciously.

The candle that he brought made a nice centerpiece as we talked well into the night. Father Dulante told me that both he and Louis were conspiring to move Isabel back into Louis' own castle so that she could be safe from Father Raphael. It was a delicate situation. Even though she was still Louis' sister, Isabel was a servant of God and escaped marriage only by convincing the Pope that she would give her life to her servitude.

That meant that she belonged to the church to some unspoken degree. If Father Raphael had the Pope's ear as well as we suspected this could lead to something we were not prepared for.

The two of us were silent for several long minutes and Father Dulante stood up to leave. I felt a sudden rush of panic and I admit that I did not want to be left alone here. I grabbed his arm quickly before I realized what I had done and Father Dulante's eyes grew worried.

"What is it, Marciel?" he asked.

"I – I need to show you something." I whispered.

The tone of my voice must've alerted him because he turned to look over his shoulder to be sure there was no one at the door and moved in closer toward me so that we could whisper.

"Marco, there is something you should know" I began, "it will not be easy for you but you're the only one I trust."

Father Dulante was taken aback by my familiar use of his first name and nodded while placing his hands on either of my arms. He looked directly into my eyes as he spoke, emphasizing his sincerity.

"You can tell me anything" he said softly, "not only as a priest but as your friend."

I wanted to break down right there but I just smiled in relief and led him toward my bed and pulled it out. I handed him the book and sat down on the bed. It had all the answers in it. Everything and anything I had been through since my arrival on earth he would know it because I had the power to reveal the words to him even though they were written in angelic script.

Father Dulante began to read and once he got deep within the first paragraph, found he needed to sit down though he never lifted his eyes off the pages. His jaw went slack and his hand covered his mouth while holding the large book's cover in the other hand. I saw the tears fall from his eyes and I could feel the emotion overtaking him as he was exposed to what was written in such sacred text.

I dared not go to him. Not yet. I needed to see whether he would accept it or call it heresy. Some mortals did not take things as easy as you would think. Some were so overwhelmed that they knew how to do nothing else but to lash out. Their minds could not comprehend what I was revealing in a single moment, to Father Dulante and I could only have faith that that his could. And pray he would not feed me to the wolves.

The centerpiece candle was burning down to the wick when Father Dulante finished. He took in a deep, shaky, breath and lifted his wet, puffy eyes to me. I knew what he was searching for. Some sort of confirmation that I was indeed the angelic being I claimed to be. Here I was standing before him as a human. No wings, no heavenly halo. Just a man, same as he.

He tore his eyes from me and looked to the table where the jug sat that the Lord had praised me on. His hands gingerly reached for it, pulling it closer to his chest. Very gently, he lifted it to eye level and studied the scene I'd carved into it before turning to me again.

"Is this…the piece of work that the Lord complimented you on?" he asked.

"Yes." I said.

"The Lord…touched this with his own hands?"

"Yes." I said again. "Sitting in the same seat you are in now, we shared the water together and talked as you and I do, now."

He brought the jug to his lips and closed his eyes, kissing it, reverently. I was filled with empathy for him. I wanted to comfort him but I could not. I was losing my faith and it had been so long since I'd seen my Lord that I felt a bit resentful toward him.

Lowering my head I stared down at the floor while Father Dulante took it all in. I had very little to offer him besides that book and secretly I was hoping that he would not ask me for anything else.

"I will help you. What do you need of me?" he said, breaking from his thoughts.

"I need you to know that this book is here in the event" I paused, lifting my eyes to meet his again, "in the event that something happens to me."

He didn't believe what I said, I could tell by the look in his eyes, and then it dawned on him, suddenly. He knew I was afraid, and that there was something worthy of my fear. He hadn't pieced it together entirely, yet and I wasn't going to fill him in.

"Have you told –"

"I haven't told anyone else." I broke in.

He nodded and looked back down at the book, running his fingers over the lettering and the leather binding. I could tell that he was afraid, too. He had every reason to be. I knew that this would get much worse before it got better. The problem was that I had no idea what Isabel had to do with any of this. What would God and Lucifer need with this mortal woman? And why was I chosen?

They were answers I may never get but I was not going to have all I'd done be in vain. If I died, then my words would be protected. The events would be documented and perhaps one day would serve as answers.

I found the strength to stand up and I walked to where Father Dulante sat. Crouching before him so that he and I were eye to eye, I lay my hand on his shoulder and whispered quietly to him.

"I'm afraid that the knowledge I've given to you could be dangerous. Maybe even endanger your life." I explained. "You must know this before you take on such a burden."

"I will take up any cross for my Lord." Father Dulante said with no hesitation in his voice.

I admired him even more right there. He did not ask why. He did not question the motives. He just wanted to serve the Lord and if his life was to be used or sacrificed for that cause then he was willing to lay it down.

I felt a weight lifted off my shoulders to know that I was not alone in this. No matter what happened, I would not be forgotten. The feeling of camaraderie I felt with him was strong; he was my friend. I was fond of many people that I met on my journey but this was different. I trusted him with my secrets and my life.

I could tell that he felt the same way and I embraced him in a brotherly hug. I had not felt the touch of another in this way since the Lord came to me and I realized I was not only struggling with my faith, I was lonely. I had no contact with my brothers in Heaven, no more long talks with the Lord, no songs to fill my soul like the ones of angels. The choir that Father Dulante led was, as I mentioned before, the closest thing to it.

"We must act fast" I said quietly as I pulled from his embrace, "I do not know how much time we have left or.. I have left."

The words seemed to really trouble him as I spoke them. His eyes studied me for a long moment before nodding and lowering his voice to a barely audible whisper.

"I will converse with Louis and we will devise a way for us all to meet together. You formulate a plan and we'll help you execute it."

He sighed and looked around again and the worry caused his brow to crease again. He was looking much older these days as I'm sure we all were.

"You were right, Marciel. There is danger here. There is evil in the house of the Lord."

"We will fight it, Marco" I said, "together."

He smiled and I returned it just the same before we both walked to the door. He slipped a copy of the key to my room into my hand then held up a spare with a wink then stood outside my door as I closed it. I could hear him lock it and quickly disappear down the hall.

I went back to my desk turning it over, then using the sealing wax to adhere my key to the bottom I pressed the metal into before adding more seal just to be safe. I wasn't sure for how long or how well it would hold up but it was the only place I could think of at the time. Setting the desk upright again, I neatly arranged the papers to their original position and then sat down. I had to think of a plan. They were counting on me, and so was Isabel. I didn't even want to think of what would happen if my plan failed.

It had been days since I knelt down and prayed. I looked over at the jug that Father Dulante was holding earlier. The emotion that filled him as he touched the item that the Lord had touched not even a week ago played once more in my mind. I wanted to feel like that again.

I stood up and walked over to the table and picked up the jug, running my thumb over the etched, wooden scene. Closing my eyes I brought it to my chest and held it like a dying child. All I could feel was loss. I was slipping away from Heaven a little further every day. I couldn't help but wonder if I would remember anything I once knew. Already my memory of Heaven dwindled until most of my memories were consumed with the mortal life I had been living for the past few years.

NOVEMBER 8, 1226: MIRIAM'S INTERLUDE

Miriam ran through her mother's chambers, giggling as she chased her Kitten, Pierre. The long-haired, white feline meow'd and lead her through the maze of clawed feet beneath tables and chairs while the two played. Skittering over rugs and regaining their footing over polished marble floors, the duo stopped at the distant sound of heavy footfalls approaching. Pierre's hair bristled and outward and down his spine, causing it to arch and contract, and with a low, quiet hiss he began to retreat into the shadowed corner behind the furniture.

Miriam's hazel eyes grew larger at the sound, which grew ever-louder and shook the brass hardware of the door. Each stomp of booted heel felt heavier and heavier with evident hostility laced through the cadence. Miriam's mother, Anjolie, was just coming out of her dressing room when she, too, heard it. The sound caused the small, nimble woman to freeze before reacting instantaneously. Without hesitation she grabbed her cloak and tossed it over the chaise where Miriam huddled, revealing to the small girl the look of panic rising in the otherwise calm and serene woman.

Falling to her knees, Anjolie looked her daughter squarely in the eyes, "Miriam!" She demanded her daughter's attention.

Miriam had never heard a harsh word out of her mother and was suddenly in full attention, dragging her gaze from the door that seemed to grow larger and larger as the sound of the boots thumped closer.

"Do not make a sound." Miriam's eyes began to fill with tears but her mother sought to ease her without losing the importance of her directions.

"No matter what you hear, you remain silent. Do you hear mommy?"

Still frozen in fear, Miriam remained silent. Anjolie, growing desperate and out of time nudged her daughter with push of her tiny shoulder, rousing her back to the sound of her voice, "Promise, Miriam!"

Miriam's heart was beating so fast and she was starting to tremble, but she looked into her mother's eyes and nodded. Even in the moment of impending danger, her mother smiled warmly at her. The strands of her mother's chocolate hair fell to the floor, shielding the light for a moment. Anjolie pulled her daughter's small hand to her lips, kissing it gently before pushing the little girl back further. Miriam crept backwards until her back hit the cool wall and her leg tickled at the sensation of Pierre's fur. Anjolie's face disappeared and the hem of her cloak replaced the light, leaving Miriam and Pierre in darkness.

When Anjolie stood, her fingers tightened around the rosary strung around her neck, then turned and faced the door. The thunderous sound of footfalls came to an abrupt stop outside the door just as the wood cracked and splintered around the edges. The force of the blow from the other side was so powerful, the oak bowed in the center before bursting inward. The hinges gave way, leaving the broken wood to hang limply to the side.

The stern visage of the Duke broke through the ranks of the men staring accusingly at her, breaking the short-lived silence with his announcement, "The King is dead."

Anjolie cried out and began to fall to her knees in disbelief, "No!"

She didn't understand. Her King, her lover was dead? She had no time to process the first announcement before the second fell upon her ears.

“We are ordered by the Queen to take you into custody for the murder of the King and treason against her Majesty!” The Duke snarled at her before his arm jutted out and he pointed at her. “Sieze her! Bring her to Lord Augustine’s prison holding for questioning.”

Anjolie struggled against the hands of the men, “No!”

It was useless, she knew. No one would believe her.

As the Duke turned, he made his way back through the opening ranks of men before speaking over his shoulder, “Find her daughter Miriam. She is to be taken out of the Kingdom, exiled into Corsican’s Orphanage.”

Anjolie screamed out in protest again, trying to rip free of her captors. Corsican’s Orphanage was prison full of sickness, travesty and the short lived lives of the children condemned to its walls. The men drug her from the chambers and began marching her down the hall to her fate, while the others stormed down toward the Nursemaid’s chambers.

In the commotion, Perla had rushed toward Anjolie’s chambers through the secret entrance but came too late. The men were already there. She stood trembling in the dark, hidden hallway waiting for the men to leave. When there was silence, the woman pushed open the door and held her breath hoping that there was no one waiting. She squeezed through the small opening one leg at a time before looking around, and seeing no one, fell to her knees calling out in a whisper for Miriam.

"Mon petite!" Perla knew that Miriam liked to hide beneath the furniture. She looked under the grand couch with its frilly skirt.

There was no sign of Miriam, so she crawled further but she was so afraid the men would come back, causing her panic to pour out into her voice, "S'il vous plait! Come to me!"

Miriam's muffled cry finally reached Perla's ears and she gasped, rushing toward the chaise lounge, flipping Anjolie's cloak away from the floor. Peering down, she saw the frightened face of the little girl she'd raised since infancy flush with fright. Tear stained cheeks were matted with her hair and the soft fur of Pierre who she clutched in her chubby little hands. Perla let out a sigh of relief and waved for her to come.

"Quickly, mon petite!" She reached in and grabbed the girl's arm, sliding her under the chaise and into her arms.

Miriam was three when it happened. But the nightmares never went away. Never grew distant. She remembered every detail of her mother's face that day. Even weeks later, still on the run with Perla, she woke up in a fit of night terrors -- shaking, wet, and soiled – frozen in a catatonic state of terror. It would be hours before her rigid limbs would bend again, allowing her to fall into a fitful sleep. Word finally reached them through the drunken rumors of the soldiers who gave no mind of the words that poured like the ale they spilled through filthy lips. Anjolie was tortured and beheaded at the Queen's behest and they were now scouring the lands in search of the runaway nursemaid and the girl.

Huddled behind the barrels of wine and ale, the girls risked life and skin to hide from the lecherous men who were seeking the bounty. The things they said made Perla ill and she held her palms against Miriam's ears for hours to try and keep the girl from hearing, as well. Many nights, the woman watched the dawn of the new day before the last slurred, wretched boasts of the men fell to drunken slumber. Another small fortune paid to the owners for their silence, and she was on her way to find the next safest shelter.

Perla and Miriam were on the road like this for two years before the nursemaid grew ill. Continuous walking, little nutrition and cold damp air through threadbare rags, gave the woman pneumonia. Her fever spiked during the night and during the day, her labored breathing made walking all but impossible. Trudging through the thick mud of a trail one evening, Perla's lungs finally caved in and she collapsed in the grass. Miriam was small and frail, no match for the weight of her caretaker, even though she was skin and bones, now. Hollow cheeks were dirty and stained with tears as she tugged at Perla's arm trying to wake her.

"Please, Madame! Please, get up. Get up!" she cried.

Perla could barely respond with anything but a groan, her body trembling with sickness. Miriam fell atop her and cradled the woman as much as she could, trying to keep her warm and safe. Exposed skin was clammy and paste-like. Her features were grey, and her lips turning blue. The woman's breaths were growing weak and shallow. Miriam thought she would die, right here in the middle of nowhere and leave her all alone in the world. The girl closed her eyes and prayed, as it was the only thing she could really do. They had nothing. There was no water, no food, no weapons or healing herbs. The two hadn't eaten in days.

"Please don't die, Madame!" Miriam's body shook with her sobs and she raised her pointed chin to the sky, "God, please don't take her."

Miriam's eyes gave in to the exhaustion and grew too heavy to hold open any longer. Sleep made its way into her and she slipped into the cold waters of sleep. She awoke to the sound of hooves clopping. Not knowing if it was real, she tried to look around but her sight was blurry and dim. The only thing she could see was the vapor of her breath against some light that swung back and forth against a black sky.

"I'm dead." She uttered weakly.

"Not yet," a voice responded before the shadow leaned down and the face of an old woman appeared, "God has not seen fit to take ye, just yet."

She had the kindest face that Miriam had ever seen. It was round and plump with rosy cheeks, and her eyes glittered when they crinkled.

The old woman rose up again and nodded to someone on her left. "Gather her up."

The light once more gave way to another face, the man that appeared was equally weathered in age, as the woman's. He leaned in and wrapped his wiry arms around Miriam, lifting her with just a hint of strain. The girl may be small, but he was old.

“Let’s get ye out of the cold, Lass.” He let out a small groan as his spine straightened up and he cradled her into his tattered, meager coat.

Miriam realized that she almost forgot about Perla, which gave an ache to her heart. She croaked out a call to her nursemaid, “Perla..!” but her bony arm was too weak to hold itself up for long.

“Shh, Lass.” The old man soothed.

Miriam’s head lolled to the side and she caught a glimpse of the woman’s body being hefted into the cart. She could not tell if she was dead or alive. The strain on Miriam’s throat from calling out to Perla made her cough, violently. Each breath she took inside felt like she was inhaling splinters of glass that scraped away at the delicate tissue of her lungs.

The older woman threw her own cloak around the girl and waved her arm toward the covered portion of the carriage, “Put her in the back with the furs. We must get back, quickly.”

There were several others riding along, but Miriam did not see their faces. She could only hear their voices muffled through her semiconscious state. The steady back and forth rocking of the carriage sealed her fate; she was deep asleep within minutes.

It was days of Miriam slipping in and out of fever induced sleep. She hallucinated and screamed out in the middle of the night, calling out names of people that were never there. She was always soaked with fever that needed constant cool rags to break. There were incidents of her trying to fight off those that were there to help, her eyes wide and wild – seeing yet unseeing. Whatever it was that she saw, was not what her attendants could account for. When they would get her calm down and she fell back to the bed, her eyes stared off into the distance and she muttered about nonsense, at first. As the days carried on, her visions grew more frightening. She muttered the names of angels, of God's wrath and even seemed to speak with the Blessed Mother. The attendants were too scared to sit with her now and so they went and told the old nun that saved her, Lydia.

Lydia argued that she was struck with fever and could not possibly be seeing the things she described but the attendants wanted no part of it, any longer. Lydia would have to tend to the girl, herself. Dismissing the woman in front of her, she sent her back to her room for the night.

"I'll see to the Lass m'self. Get some rest. I'll see you in the mornin'." Lydia stood slowly and grabbed her walking stick, making her way slowly toward the girl's room. Just outside the door, she lit the candle and paused, hearing the girl speaking in hushed tones. Lydia listened for a moment thinking the poor thing was in the midst of another fever. She was about to enter when she heard another voice.

The woman was startled at first, then angry. She had sent the other attendant to bed after she had refused to look after the girl, now she was back? Nudging the door open with the end of the stick, Lydia stopped and gasped. A woman sat at the edge of the bed, her hand cupping the small girl's and smiled down at her. The very sight of her made Lydia's heart swell with love so great, that she felt as if it was enough for the whole world. The intensity of the emotion caused her to buckle slightly and put more weight down on the stick. She realized then that there was no light in the room, it was the glow around the woman that filled up the room like a thousand candles.

The two had stopped talking, then and the glowing woman leaned in to kiss Miriam's cheek. Standing upright slowly, she allowed her gaze to rest upon Lydia. The gaze was deep and warm, filling her chest with flames of compassion that instantly made the old woman weep. She could barely utter the words, but managed, feebly.

"Hail..Mary.." she began, and had to catch her breath between sobs, "full of grace."

The woman walked towards her and Lydia fell to one knee, dropping her gaze acquiescingly to the Mother of God. The hem of the Virgin's skirts came to rest in front before the Holy Mother continued walking and went right through her.

The feeling was so intense that the old woman let out a loud groan. It felt as if her soul burst into the sun like small drops of rain evaporating off the petal of a flower. Each molecule was captured in mid-air, pausing as time stood still and the light blinded her. She could not move, nor speak. When she took in a breath, time sped to catch up and she felt each molecule return. Each tiny raindrop was the tears of the world, and each tear brought all the anguish, hope, love and worry that accompanied it.

Lydia gulped in the air but realized, she was unable to see. She had literally, looked into the sunlight that was the most Holy of all women. From that day, she would never regain her sight. Long after she had passed, to this very day, others have claimed to see the blind old woman tending to the roses of the garden. Roses that would not wither or die, even when the building had crumpled and fell to the earth from decay and time. Roses that deflected the strangling vines of weeds and the mastication by jaws of scavengers and insects.

Miriam was standing in that garden now as the memories came flooding back. A voice behind her brought her back into the conversation she fell out of without notice.

"Mon petite?" Perla said the words softly, reaching out for her shoulder.

Gazing down at her hands, a few tears made their way down Miriam's cheek and she handed the habit to her nursemaid. Now a woman, Miriam could only thank God that she still had Perla after nearly losing her, that fateful night. Now older, a little more wrinkles at the corners of her eyes, Perla helped Miriam get ready for morning prayers.

"Miriam, the burden is great. I know this." She whispered as gently as she could. "But it is through this sacrifice that we show our love to God. He saved you, and you must save others. This is our lesson, and our journey. Grace be to Him, that we lived to see this day, and every day after."

“Yes, Madame. I know.” Miriam nodded, softly. “It does not pain me to love her. It was not She that killed my mother.”

Perla paused at the words, before gently smoothing out the black robe. She whispered lower this time, in an almost chastising tone, “Never say those words, again. No one must know. Only you, and I, and God.”

Miriam’s eyes fell once more to gaze at her own feet and did not meet her nursemaid’s again until after morning prayers, “Yes, Madame.”

The nursemaid was as close as Miriam would ever have to a mother in this lifetime. Her own had suffered a terrible fate at the Queen’s hand. In Miriam’s mind, the King’s hands were just a full of blood. He knew that the Queen was a resolute woman who would never stand down from acquiring the power and throne for her son. In turn, it kept the Queen in power, as well. To the public the Queen was pious and chaste, serving God through prayer, alms to the poor and attending church often. She raised her children by the strict disciplines of the Catholic Church.

In turn, this left the King’s earthly desires unquenched. He saw the beauty and grace of Miriam’s mother and pursued her relentlessly until she gave in. He never backed out of his promises to her. She had a lavishly furnished apartment in the castle, opposite the wing that the Queen stayed in. He made sure to stock her purse full of gold and her skin adorned in every jewel he could find, near and far. The Queen's jealousy grew and festered, until finally, Anjolie was with child. The Queen dismissed the pregnancy and laughed. The King would never recognize a bastard child. Not with her own, noble-birth children to secure his lineage and rule.

But when Miriam was born, and the King looked down upon her eyes, he loved her as much as he loved her mother, his consort. He reached out for her and cradled her small head in his hand then lowered himself to the bed and wept. Anjolie thought something was wrong and reached for him, scared that she hadn't seen a disfiguration or sickness in the babe.

"No," he whispered, "nothing is wrong. She is perfect. A gift from God, above."

Word spread like wildfire at his words. The king did not care, but the Queen roared so loud, it shook the stones of the castle, itself. She sent cups and paintings crashing into the stone walls, at the servants, the ladies-in-waiting, her Councilmen who had come to talk sense into her.

It nearly drove her mad. The King tried to see her that night and she threw herself into another fit of rage. The two screamed at one another for hours, until exhausted, he vowed never to share her bed again, until she be tame and reasonable.

When the King left, she sat in the center of the room, her eyes taking in the shambles and ruin. Something moved. She caught it out of the corner of her eye. Her fury was tempered by her curiosity. Who would be so bold to sneak into her bedchambers unannounced?

She called out to the intruder, having no fear of an assassin or threat upon her life, "You dare come to me without invitation? Show yourself to me."

The Queen did not move to face the presence. Instead, she lifted her chin and waited. Waited to be shown proper respect by whoever it was. Expecting no less, she spoke not another word until it seemed to slither along the far side of the wall, jumping from shadow to shadow until, from the darkness, a man emerged slowly into the light.

The Queen steadied herself. His presence seemed to suffocate what little light tried to illuminate his features. The irises of his eyes were so black, she felt like she was staring into the abyss. Something within her *knew*. In some primordial way, this was Evil.

And she did not care.

Jealousy crept into her heart and turned it black. Straightening her spine, she steeled her trembling hands by clasping them behind her back, “Who are you?”

The man bowed deeply with unearthly grace. His long coat whipped out behind him and he gazed up at her. “A *humble* servant.”

The Queen narrowed her gaze at the man. Waiting.

“Call me, Raphael.”

THE GEMINI - MIRIAM

Isabel lay quietly on the bed and Louis slept across from her on the chair near the door. Miriam came in and placed a blanket over him then paused as he stirred, careful not to wake him. It was rare that Isabel was quiet like this, so sleep was a luxury that everyone took advantage of. Even Miriam herself was looking a little worn for the wear. Nights of prayer, followed by her penance dealt out by Father Raphael for her defiance to be carried out by her own hand, had left her looking years beyond her age.

Miriam vowed to God and to Isabel that she would stand by her friend's side. She knew that evil had embraced this otherwise holy place for whatever reason. That reason was not hers to question. God's plan was beyond human comprehension. She would continue to be his humble servant by ensuring that His children were kept as safe as possible.

How she had hated her so long ago. The thought crushed her heart with guilt and regret. She'd confessed every night to rhythm of the reparations against her bare flesh. So consumed by the torment of her feelings, Miriam had nearly gone mad at her own self-inflicted punishment. Falling to the floor among the blood and sweat, the past infused her memories, dragging her back into their depths again.

Gazing down at Isabel's drawn face brought her sadness, and she let her hand reach out to brush the back of her knuckles over the sharp hill of her cheekbone. Isabel stirred slightly, turning toward the warmth generated by those fingers. Miriam's breath caught suddenly at how cold her friend's skin was. It sent a deeper chill within her and she pulled her hand back to rub at her arms, subconsciously pulling her shawl tighter around her shoulders.

Turning to glance around the room, Miriam found the discarded blanket from the foot of Isabel's bed that she must have kicked off and reached over to grab it. She could feel the temperature in the room drop even more and she stopped mid-bend. On the air before her, her breath hung there. She felt like a child suddenly; afraid to peek under the bed where the blanket was bunched up.

Forcing her lips to close, she swallowed back the fear and snatched the blanket quickly with her eyes closed, then turned to place it on Isabel only to be stopped abruptly. She let out a short scream when she collided with Isabel who was now standing beside the bed and directly in front of her.

"Isabel! You frightened me!" She said, breathlessly.

Isabel responded by tipping her head slowly to the side, her darkened eyes never leaving Miriam's but seeming to be looking past her. Miriam took a step back and tried to smile but a foul smell began to roll off her friend's breath. It was more than Miriam could stand and she had to cover her nose with her hand. A feeling of nausea welled up within her and she placed her hand on the bed to steady herself.

Before she knew what happened, Isabel reached out and ensnared Miriam's hair between her fingers, jerking her head to the side and cocking her face upward so that she was forced to stare up into Isabel's features which were turning both malignant and vile. The younger woman began to flail in surprise and yelped in protest. She called out for Louis who was still sleeping in the chair nearby.

"Louis! Help me!" Fear escalated the shrill of her scream and filled the room.

Unable to turn her face, she stared up in horror as she watched Isabel's eyes roll back into her head and her mouth open wide. Her teeth and her tongue were so black it looked like she drank a bottle of liquid ash. Miriam struggled harder, digging her heels into the floor. She kicked and punched against the un-moving frame of her friend who was transforming right before her very eyes into a demonic nightmare.

Isabel's jaw continued to open wider and Miriam began to cry. She could hear the joint dislocating and the lower portion of her bone unhinging and falling down to her chest while stretching the skin unnaturally.

"No!" Miriam screamed out again, praying it would snap Isabel out of this trance or wake Louis up from his deep sleep to help her.

Miriam's scream gave Isabel opportunity to slip her fingers into her mouth and hold it open. Tilting her head downward, gave Miriam a better view of writhing nest of maggots that began pouring from Isabel's mouth into her own. Miriam gagged and pounded her fists harder as flies began buzzing angrily about, accosting her face and eyes.

Louis, meanwhile, was dream-state far away from the terrors of the Abbey and Isabel. Back in the fields of his homeland, he rode the steed beneath him, leading the hunt. It was his first time. The freedom was unlike anything he'd ever experienced in his whole life. The wind was sweeter, and the thrill was more exhilarating at the front line.

Leaning forward he pushed onward, feeling the power of the beast's flanks between his legs. Nostrils flared, and the vapor of the heated breath on winter's air curled around the rising low-lying fog. The two danced, fighting for dominance. The thunder of the animal's hooves clapped in time with the beating of his heart and Louis finally caught sight of it! Simultaneously, the dogs began to bark furiously and take off beneath the brush toward the prize. Louis could feel the horse pull back and he grew angry, driving his spurred heels into its hind quarters.

From a short distance away one of the dogs let out a horrific shriek and the horse reared up and back. Louis held on as tight as he could double wrapping his hands in the reigns and squeezing his thighs, stubbornly. He could almost hear his riding instructor chastising him in the back of his mind but pride was a tricky thing.

The front hooves of the horse fell to the earth again and Louis tried to regain control. The leather reigns had torn up the skin between his fingers and he could feel the blood, even as he pulled and jerked, attempting to redirect his mount. Out of nowhere, the body of one of the hounds was thrown, knocking Louis from where he sat.

Falling to the floor, he was jolted from the dream and finally connected the screams from Miriam to the scene the played out before him. He almost wished he was back asleep when his mind processed that what he was seeing was real.

Rushing to his feet, he half ran-half stumbled to Miriam's aid. Wrapping his fingers around Isabel's arm, he swung with all his might with his free hand and aimed at her temple to knock her unconscious. When his arm made contact, it succeeded in releasing Miriam from Isabel's grasp but only to refocus that ire at Louis.

Falling against the bed, Isabel righted herself by jumping into a feral crouch. Louis stood in front of Miriam and backed them both up slowly to give more distance between them. Looking into Isabel's eyes, Louis could see the absence of his sister, again. Once again, her body played host to whatever *this* was that was growling and hissing at them like some rabid animal. He was growing to hate It. To want It dead. And It could feel that.

With a dry, mocking cackle It crawled closer to him and made a sudden lunge. Louis gasped, stumbling back almost knocking Miriam over.

"Just die!" He finally cried.

"Whatever, or whoever you are…" he said warily. "Go back to Hell and leave us alone!"

Isabel cackled and lunged forward at Louis. Clawed fingers gripped his neck with the strength of four men and Louis' eyes grew large as he fought to breathe before being violently lifted off his feet. He could feel the blood circulation being cut off and hear Miriam shouting for help. Darkness was closing in when Felipe charged in and slammed the hilt of his blade into Isabel's temple resulting in her crumpling to the floor like a rag doll.

Louis sucked in a deep breath like a newborn babe taking his first breath. His hand cradled his neck gently against the coughing that caused him even more pain. There was definitely some damage; he was spitting out blood.

Father Dulante and I trailed behind moments later, running to Felipe's aid. Lifting Isabel's body from the floor they lay her onto the cot again, and Miriam pulled the blanket over her. They all seemed to fall back at the same time with a sigh of relief, exchanging glances but no words. Miriam placed her face in her palms and began to cry. I could not bear to see her in such a state. I placed my palm on her back and patted gently, offering as much comfort as I could while remaining modest and keeping her virtue out of question.

She pulled away from me abruptly and stood up to grab fresh linens and bandages. We all watched as she tended to Isabel's head wound in continued silence. She finally turned and spoke, chiding us like young boys.

"Go now. I must change her clothing and bedding."

She waved us off with a clean towel, "Shoo!"

"Fetch me some clean water and get some dinner. Why are you just sitting there?"

Her voice had a stern tone laced with anger but we all knew and we all understood. All of us were equally deprived of sleep and sanity.

"Yes mum." I said, then moved obediently to do as she asked.

Louis stared at her with fearful, tear-filled eyes. Guilt spilled over his face at the respite of being relieved of his watch duty.

Miriam glanced at Felipe and let her voice soften slightly, "Take your friend to get cleaned up and get some food in him. He'll do no good in this condition."

Felipe's jaw tightened and he nodded, curling an arm under Louis' and then helped him to his feet. He spared another look at Isabel and I could see the real thoughts he tried to hide as if he had *spoke* them aloud. That must be how the Lord saw us. Nothing was hidden to him. And staring now at Felipe I could see that he wanted nothing more than this to all end. He believed Isabel "the woman" was gone and that what was left, was evil. He believed that evil was going to destroy all of them if he didn't take matters into his own hands, soon.

I could not let him kill her.

Felipe pulled Louis to his room and helped him out of his coat. He had been through many battles with the man before him but never had he seen the defeat in his eyes that he saw now.

"Louie." He whispered roughly, shaking his friend by the shoulders.

Louis was someplace else, again.

THE CRUSADER'S INTERLUDE: LOUIS

This time he and Felipe were moving along the sand at night. Even with no sun, the grains were like shards of searing glass through their sandals. The wraps they used to blend in did no good. They were not seasoned to the environment, yet. Each step caused them to wince pain.

When the moon sat high enough above them, Louis gave indication that they were ready to make camp for the night. He and the seven other crusaders filed in and began to build what could barely be called tents from scattered palm leaves or pieces of their clothing and branches.

Two of the scouts came back moments later and informed Louis that it was safe enough to build a small campfire so the men did, and made meager rations of a meal before bunkering down for the night.

The nocturnal sounds of the desert kept Felipe alert and unable to sleep for most of the night. He was more accustomed to the sounds of the forest and its inhabitants than the eerie silence of whispering winds. Every now and then there would be a strange call of a creature he'd never heard before and his grip on the hilt of is sword would tighten.

The moon was falling into the horizon on its journey to relinquish the sky to the sun when his eyes grew so heavy he could no longer keep them open. He must've lost time – or, did he fall asleep? Time escaped him when he felt the sudden shift in wind and leapt to his feet. A spray of blood crossed his face and he watched his brother-at-arms fall without so much as a sound.

The surprise attack was so clandestine and well-timed it deserved as much awe as it did abhorrence.

Louis and Felipe were in a room in the far west wing. Father Raphael would not allow him to stay in the convent at first, insisting that it was not proper. Louis used what pull he had left with the Church to gain the upper hand. He would be allowed to stay, as deemed by the Archdiocese, but Father Raphael insisted that he be far enough out of the way to not interfere with Isabel's care. The heated debate caused alarm in the Pope and, at his insistence, a small team of his own priests were sent to escort them back. They would be reporting Isabel's progress back to him. This seemed to agitate Father Raphael all the more but he bowed his head and conceded, casting a hateful glare in Louis' direction before sweeping out of the room.

It was a long, slow ride home from the Vatican but Louis had felt a sense of accomplishment. That victory would grow dim over time. He would already see that Father Raphael had reached the other priests, winning them over. The clergy would barely speak to Louis about Isabel's condition which infuriated him. The way they were so quiet, Louis felt as though they were zombies. Their eyes seemed lifeless and grey and they would move slowly, always under Father Raphael's supervision. Louis was noticing that the two nuns looked very similar. His suspicious eye watched Miriam for days but she did not have the same demeanor. Slowly, Louis began to ease around her. The poor woman was enduring quite enough already on behalf of Isabel and him. His thoughts were heavy and racing through his weary mind, exhausting him of any reserve energy. Louis was sitting in his room across from Felipe as dusk began to fall over the earth for another night.

The tension could be felt on the air, pungent with anxiety and fear. Felipe was gazing out the window, his hands hanging loose at his sides. His breathing was slow and even but Louis could see his trusted friend and confidante were filled with thoughts. He barely spoke them since they arrived, a trait unlike him. It made Louis' heart heavy; what had he gotten him into? This was no battle with the average adversary. Louis didn't even know what they were up against.

"Speak, Felipe" he said. "I need to hear it. Whatever it is."

Felipe stood there for another long moment in silence before turning to face Louis. The two had been through so much together. Their friendship had been forged by blood, steel and honor. They were closer than brothers.

"God has left us" he said. It was so soft and plain that Louis was sure he had heard him wrong. The shock of the words left him dumb. No thoughts formed in reply to it, for what seemed like hours, but it was only seconds. If it had been any other man Louis would've been filled with rage, calling him a blasphemer. Hearing Felipe say it filled Louis with terror because it sounded so real. So very, very real. When Louis finally found his tongue, his voice was stretched and frail, "By all things holy, I pray that is not the truth."

Lowering his head, Louis looked down to the book in his hands. It was a small parchment that he carried with him. In times when he felt his fear against a sea of soldiers, during odds that seemed insurmountable, this is where he found his strength. The word of God carried against his heart into every battle: “Above all, taking the shield of faith, wherewith ye shall be able to quench all the fiery darts of the wicked.”

Marciel could feel the terror gripping the entire group. The tension was thick in the air as they all sat together in the library. The Catholic Church was not lenient with those that opposed them. What they weren’t sure of was who to fear more. The constant rattling and shaking of furniture had set all of their nerves on edge. The men were jumpy and even Miriam would recoil at the slightest noise or movement. Isabel’s condition wavered between bad and worse. There were days that the situation seemed like it would improve, or that she would be alright, and other days they feared for her life. The amount of blood loss made her look feeble and pale. All the weight she had lost caused her cheeks and eyes to sink in and grow dark.

The mask over Isabel’s eyes had calmed her in the beginning like blinders on a horse, but lately it only agitated her more. She would writhe and jerk at her restraints, pulling her arms out of socket resulting in her wailing in pain. The others in the convent could take no more, and they ran out to seek shelter elsewhere in neighboring villages or abbeys. The only ones left were the ones that aided Father Raphael and Isabel's friends and family. Miriam tried her best to help the men looking after Isabel but the two nuns that were aiding Father Raphael made it nearly impossible. If Miriam was caught bringing the men extra food or clean linens she would be punished severely.

Marciel cringed every night he heard her weeping during her flagellation. And every night it seemed to last longer and longer. He admired her devotion to God and Isabel all the more because it was punishment which was required to be enforced by her very own hand. How she found the strength was beyond his comprehension. He knew, though, that it was Father Raphael's hope, and pleasure, that she would eventually give in.

Louis was growing fatigued in his faith, as well as, physically. The men could barely console him most days as he'd wake from monstrous nightmares, cursing and denouncing God for what he was putting his sister through.

"This is too much!!" he'd scream to the skies, and Felipe would try to keep him from attacking those around him.

There were days he'd rush the door, aiming his hate toward Father Raphael, sword drawn. It was those nights that the men had to be most vigil. Louis never gave any warning so they had to be on their best guard. It was on one of those nights when they were struggling to wrestle the Templar's weapon from his white-knuckled grasp that they heard the most ungodly scream of all. Dropping his weapon, he rushed past Marciel and the other two to his sister's door only to have it slammed shut in his face with such violence that the frame cracked and pushed inward. Louis tugged frantically at it while the others tried to catch up to him.

"ISABEL!" he cried, his voice cracked and straining against his throat. "No..Not again!"

SECRET TO THE END - MARCIEL

Marciel nearly shrunk back at the amount of torment in Louis' voice. Afraid of what was beyond the door, flashbacks of the last time filled his head causing the bile in his stomach to crawl upwards from the depths of his belly. Behind him, Father Dulante stopped dead in his tracks and Felipe barreled through them to help his brother-in-arms. The two men were nearly clawing at the door to wedge it free but it was sealed shut. The floor beneath them trembled and Isabel howled once more – a mix of human and in-human vocals reaching their spinal cords, traveling down to their knees. They all paused until their struggle returned with more urgency than before.

Seeing how futile their attempts were, they cowered back as the room before them seemed to go silent and take a breath, pulling the door inward until it splintered and broke. The pieces exploded throughout the room, some of the sharper pieces embedding in the men's skin. They were undeterred by the danger, however, and all of them pushed against one another to the horrific scene before them.

Louis' body lurched forward and his back hunched while he grabbed at the nearest piece of furniture to steady himself. His companion Felipe, the large, stoic man with the eyes of a lion was forced to step back. Father Dulante and I were frozen where we stood even as the stench of Louis' sickness filled the room.

"My God.." was all I could manage to say.

I could feel my entire body shaking at the scene in front of me. How could this all be real? Isabel was hunched in a corner near a wall stained with blood and feces. Crouched low, she looked like a feral stray, with the fluids matted in her hair and on her face. She was shoving something in her mouth. I couldn't figure out what it was – no, I refused to process what it was – until finally, realization hit me. She turned and faced us, the ugly mask that covered her eyes only accentuating the demonic grin on her features.

Her side was wide open and half of her intestines were oozing through the open wound. She was eating her own flesh! Louis was still emptying his stomach when Felipe finally lost it and drew his sword. "I will end this. We have to put her down and end this is MADNESS!"

Louis who was on his knees, now, grabbed Felipe's ankle and cried out, "NO!" but Felipe was pulling away in disregard. Tearing my eyes from Isabel, I reached out for Felipe to restrain him causing Father Dulante to snap out of his shock and help. Isabel seemed amused by it all in some sick, twisted way. She skittered along the floor like a spider, even using her back leg to rest against the wall as if perching on her web. Her entrails dragging alongside her, she cackled and hissed at us. The smell of death and feces, mixed with the coppery taint of blood made our stomachs turn, again.

I had no clue what to do.

It was Father Dulante who surprised us all and came into the scene with the fire of God behind him. Rushing forward, he thrust his hand out wielding the cross that dangled from around his neck.

"Unclean thing, it is by the power of the almighty God who commands you now to hear him and obey his command!" The priest continued forward cautiously, knowing how clever and dangerous the Devil was.

Isabel let out a cry from Hell and arched her back like a wolf howling at the moon. The sound made our ears ache and the floor to rumble. With our balance thrown off, I fell back into Louis who had lost all the color in his features but Father Dulante radiated with his newfound faith in the power of God. He faced this beast head on with no regard for his own safety.

Felipe stood behind him with his sword at the ready. His knuckles were pink and white from strain. With every step the Priest took, Felipe matched it stride for stride. *It's working!* I thought to myself then pushed off Louis to help the two corralling Isabel to the far wall until she had nowhere else to go.

Isabel lurched forward, clawed fingers swiping at them like a cornered rat. Her back hunched and she panted loudly, eyeing them and sizing them up. When Father Dulante brought out the vial of Holy Water she turned her face away and cringed. A flurry of ancient words flew from her lips in the voices of many souls, not just one. The other two men could not understand the language but Marciel did.

"Kill the Priest! *He will kill us!* Send him to Hell! *Shove that cross in his ass!* He's killing us! *Father save us!* She's ours! *Take her with us!*"

Marciel's eyes widened with fear, but Father Dulante splashed the blessed water across repeatedly until she collapsed on the floor. Felipe did not hesitate to subdue her. He threw a blanket over her body and pinned her to the floor.

"She's DEAD!" Louis was on the verge of a meltdown and continued to shout the words from his spot on the floor.

I found a sheet that was strewn across the room and wound it tightly into a rope then began to bind Isabel within the blanket. Felipe's eyes were locked on her form, ready to strike in an instant. She might be dead, but I did not say it. If she was her soul was lost to the Beast, forever. *Please, my God, don't let this be.*

"Let's get her into a bed and get the surgeon. Quickly, Louis! Fetch the surgeon or she WILL die, certainly!"

Louis scrambled to his feet and ran out the door. Father Dulante kept close watch on Isabel with his crucifix held out before him like a beacon while Felipe and I wrangled her to the bed. The three of us stood there over her mangled body and wept.

After a long few moments, Louis ran back into the room with the surgeon before the unsuspecting man entered. He so stunned at her condition he nearly fell over himself in a dead stop once he passed the threshold. Louis shoved him impatiently toward his sister and the three of us slid away to let him work.

The doctor worked as fast as he could with a look of hopelessness. He had never seen anything so heinous throughout his whole career. He'd seen war, plague and murder but nothing could prepare him for what he had to do, now.

The last stitch in place, he slid the sheet over the woman's body and turned so that he faced the four men, whispering, "It is my guess that she will not live long."

Louis let out a groan and covered his face with his arm. The three of us remaining let the tears fall silently while we listened.

"I don't know who – or what – did this to her but it is a miracle that she was still breathing when I arrived. Infection will set in and she will suffer. May God have mercy on her and take her sooner than later."

The surgeons head dropped and he rushed out, leaving us with the remnants of the beautiful Isabel. Looking at her from where we stood, she appeared for a brief moment to be sleeping – *dare I think it?* – peacefully.

BROKEN - ISABEL

Being held captive in her own body she was tired and battered and had had no idea how to fight the evil she was possessed with. She could hear the whispers night and day. The voices kept her awake even when she looked like she was asleep. Knowing she had to reserve her strength, she'd eat whenever she could and sleep when they'd let her.

The weakness had taken its toll on her. She needed Miriam's constant assistance but knowing that the woman endured punishment for her every kindness, made Isabel overcome with guilt. The voices played with her fears, building them up, and using them against her. She was sure that Miriam would die for helping her unless Isabel could fight through this. When she was able to pray, the spirits within her would scream and make her ill, but she never gave in. She would let her family know she was still there. Somewhere. It took all her strength to move. Broken and bruised bones made it nearly impossible but she would exert all her will to move and signal those waiting beside her.

Sometimes she could hear their voice. So different than those in her head, and so far away, it was all she could do not to drown in despair. The sting of her fingertips throbbed with the missing skin and fingernails that no longer protected the nerves. Her throat burned from the constant screaming and howling. She didn't understand why God allowed this to happen to her but she had faith that it would all be revealed if she remained steadfast and devout.

The temptation to believe that he had forsaken her were strong on some days, but she held fast to the fact that, that was exactly what Lucifer would have her believe. Marciel's presence was always felt whenever he was near. Her heart and soul was convinced that he would somehow be the one to save her from all this. Perhaps, all this was for him? She'd sigh inwardly, at the thought. It was just conjecture. Simple guesses. No sign had been given to the meaning of this all but she knew that God had a plan. He would not give her more than she could endure. Even if he desired her to come home to Him – all of this would not be in vain.

It was those thoughts that gave her the strength. But the Beast was persistent. He'd growl and laugh within her, chiding her ridiculous thoughts.

"Dear Isabel, do you not see?" his smooth voice purred against her ear.

From outside, Louis was on watch never to leave her bed. He would see his sister's head twitch to the side. The former Knight was a shadow of his former glory as he leaned forward.

"Isss-abel" this time the Beast rolled the "s" off the tip its tongue as if savoring the sound of it in his mouth.

Isabel focused her thoughts and silently recited a prayer of protection. The Devils laugh roared in her head and she could feel her ears burning in pain. Being jerked up suddenly, she listened helplessly as Louis shouted for help.

The Beast gave her sight behind the mask and she was forced to watch while her spirit floated above her body which was being maneuvered like a rag-doll. She stood rigid now, before her brother. The fear on her sibling's face made her weep from within. He tried to reach her but was pinned to his chair, unable to move.

Forced to watch the systematic torture of his sister, Louis was losing the battle and hold on his sanity. The usual scent of Jasmine was replaced by the pungent stench of sulfur and death. Isabel's head twitched into awkward positions and stubby fingers reached upward to Heaven before the unseen whip cracked against the air and found its home against her back. The skin already fragile, ripped like dry parchment. Bone and cartilage could be seen as she flinched, causing the blood to spill.

The unearthly voices cried out again from her mouth, "Save her!" they chanted, mockingly.

"This one is OURS! She will be a whore in Hell!" Each heinous outburst caused Louis to moan in agony, defenseless to do anything but watch. He struggled with all of his might but it was futile. He might as well have been pinned by the Earth itself. Another lash and the flesh of Isabel's back peeled and rolled down, hanging there. More lashes cracked through the air, tenderizing the muscle of the frail woman, dealing its irreversible damage.

Louis' sanity finally broke. He thrashed and cursed, pulling against the imaginary binds that kept him glued to the chair. He felt scratches and bites tearing at his flesh and screamed out until blood filled his throat and his voice was lost in a gurgle. The candles that were lit around the room fueled with the rage and fear, shot upward like pyres and filled the room with blazing heat and light. It looked like the room itself was on fire. Louis turned his head to shield himself from it and from the corner of his eye saw Father Raphael emerge from the lapping flames untouched. The slender man's robes were alive around him and the wooden crucifix that swung from around his neck was now facing downward. Blood dripped down with each cadence of his steps from the weeping eyes of the Lord.

Louis tried to back up and push his chair away but he couldn't. He was a trapped, caged animal at the mercy of this unholy man. The slick smile of the approaching priest was like oil against his features, he was there to initiate more pain and humiliation to the siblings who had been faithful and loving servants of God. Behind him, Louis noticed movement and though all sense told him not to look, he could not help it. The two nuns and the clergy of Vatican priests proceeded in and on their heels, the most hideous creatures he'd ever seen; hellhounds. Their muzzles swung low with serrated teeth that gnashed and snapped at the scent of Louis.

Louis could feel his bladder empty, filling the room with the stench of his urine. The Hellhounds were roused by it, tugging against the large chains that drug behind them. Father Raphael slid his hand through the mane of one and it sat obediently, still growling in Louis' direction.

"Not now, Zelios. He must watch first then you shall have your snack." The hound hunched down digging talons into the stone floor beneath it. Its maw salivated at the prospect of having Louis' flesh within its grasp.

The two nuns moved forward and dropped their robes, standing shoulder to shoulder before the dark priest. Their bodies were covered in scars and lacerations that still wept with infection due to neglect. Their dry, cracked lips pulled back in deviant smiles, both vying for their Master's attention. Meanwhile, Isabel still hung in the air just out of reach of the crackling flames that stretched toward her, wanting to engulf her. When Father Raphael turned his attention away from the twin Harlots, they hissed and wailed in jealousy.

The clergy of males moved behind Isabel and lined up awaiting his command. It was that single wave of his hand that signaled them to begin. They moved forward and ripped her ragged clothing off, violently, giving no care for the fresh wounds. It was so fast and careless that they took some of the hanging flesh with, discarding it on the floor with a sickening wet slap against the stone. The dark priest then turned to the Harlots and barked out a command, "The Altar."

The women once more showed their disgust at his choice and slithered off to drag the stone slab altar that sat in the corner of the room for Isabel, or her family, to pray. The items were shoved off with a sweep of their arms and landed with a crash on the floor. They didn't seem to notice as they walked through broken glass with bare feet, using inhuman strength to drag the altar into place.

Father Raphael moved to the head of the altar and one of the priests stepped forward with a chalice. Isabel's body was then dragged over and pinned to the altar. Beginning the ritual, he'd discard his robes and Louis gasped in horror at the demonic symbols and runes that were etched into his skin with black ink. They were perfect, as if they were there when he was born and part of his natural body. Father Raphael's long black hair was free and loose, hanging down past his shoulders as he chanted softly in a hushed whisper. Louis could not decipher the words.

They were no language he'd ever heard but it caused his spine to tremble and he felt the world around him bear down. The pressure in his head was enough to make him try and scream again.

The pain in his raw throat shot down the length of his neck and Louis found enough strength to struggle again. Once more, the

Hellhounds growled and snapped but never did Father Raphael waver. Isabel now seemed to gain consciousness as if waking from a dream.

Staring around her, the confusion was obvious until she pushed through the haze and realized this was really happening. All the pain and suffering she endured in her silent prison, she now had a voice and she screamed in terror, "God help me!!"

The Devil's laugh was deep and ominous as he lunged forward and grasped her by her thin neck. His lips parted and the tip of his tongue inched forward, the pink flesh dissolving into a black, forked tip that he ran over her lips. Isabel jerked and struggled to get away but she was no match for him. Shifting her gaze she caught sight of Louis and lost her will to fight. He was a broken man. Once a strong Knight of the Templars, he was a shadow of that, struggling to free him of unseen binds. The tears streamed freely from Isabel's eyes and Father Raphael hissed in pleasure. Her suffering was feeding his power. He lapped the tears up with his tongue, bringing the chalice to her face to capture a few drops before whispering down against her mouth.

"I told Father I would have you." He said. His breath was like sulfur and stung her nostrils. She didn't understand it all, this was madness. What was happening and why? He could read her thoughts, and he responded as if she spoke the words aloud to him.

"Because, Little One, it is all part of the plan." Isabel could only stare at him in horror. There was no way God would allow this to happen. She was dreaming. Yes, that was it. She was still held prisoner and the voices were tricking her. Closing her eyes, tight, she struggled to wake up and escape the scene; praying through cracked lips for God's mercy.

"Still think it's only a nightmare?" he asked, then leaned up again and handed the chalice to one of the priests beside him. They began to chant their unholy song and Father Raphael shoved open Isabel's legs. Louis' chair rocked and splintered as he fought and Isabel jolted, struggling against the hands that held her pinned down.

She screamed out in protest and choked, feeling the air cut off. Wide eyes peered up above her seeing the face of one of the Harlots who had pressed a leather strap over her throat and pressed down on either side of Isabel's head. Still struggling, Father Raphael only smiled, using his finger to trace over her pelvic bone to the stitched wound at her side. "I watched as they pierced him" he spoke, reminiscently. "His blood flowed like wine." His fingernail grew out and he snagged the stitches, ripping them open one by one. Isabel tried to pull away and cry out but she could only gather enough air to barely stay conscious.

The Hellhounds were dragging their chains closer to Louis but he didn't care. He knew he would die anyway. He kicked and rocked the chair, trying anything to break free. The more he struggled, the more damage he was dealt. Shadows converged on him, stealing fresh bites of flesh, causing the scent of blood to fill the hounds' nostrils. They were nearly in frenzy as they clawed closer.

Father Raphael, amid the fire and the chants took the chalice again and held it to Isabel's freshly open wound. The blood flowed thickly, filling it with her life. Isabel felt consciousness slipping slowly but she was not so lucky. Whenever the Harlot saw her eyes roll up, she'd release the strap, allowing precious oxygen to pour in again. The adrenaline and sudden rush of air would wake Isabel up and the strap would be tightened once more. When she got the second wind and saw the scene before her, she fought with her heart and soul, arching up off the stone slab. Father

Raphael threw his arm out, backhanding one of the priests that had lost his grip on the woman. His amusement turned to fury; Father Raphael threw his body onto Isabel and mounted her. He gave no hesitation as he thrust himself within her. The untouched woman screamed against the strap on her throat, feeling the tearing of her virginity shoot through her like a hot sword. Father Raphael let out an ungodly cry and arched his back, losing all façade of the dark priest. Flesh began to peel away like melting wax, revealing the black and red musculature of the demon within.

Louis let out one final cry and tore his arm free of the chair, leaving half the flesh of his arm behind to reach out for Isabel, "NO!"

The Hellish Beasts finally broke free of their restraints and descended upon him with the ferocity of a pack of ravenous wolves. Snarls and barks from the Alpha caused the others to cower but they continued to rip at whatever they could get of the man's body. His limbs were being pulled away; masticated within the immense jaws of the demonic beasts. Isabel was forced to watch as her brother was devoured alive, her own body being violently defiled while she bled and choked on her screams. Turning her head she caught site of the crucifix that hung on the wall and cried. Her thighs burned as the Beast continued to ravage her near lifeless form. He impaled her over and over to the chants of the men around her until she finally felt the grasp of death. She was so weak and defeated; dying would be a welcome end to this suffering.

"Sanguis bibimus" they sang, "Corpus edimus!"

The Devil, now free of human flesh watched as Isabel's eyes flickered of life. He snarled and reached over her to grab the Harlot, throwing her against the wall near the other priest. Her body broke before crumpling to the floor on top of him but still she slithered toward her Master's feet like a disfigured animal. Once free of the strap, Isabel pulled in a tattered breath and coughed violently, trying again to free herself. The Devil in his full glory now, pinned her beneath his bull-like form. Thick, sinewy muscle, sticky with discarded flesh, strained as he thrust into her again until he froze and loosed a primal howl and released his seed into her.

The walls trembled at the victorious cry but there was something else trailing behind it. Reality seemed to shudder and jump. The pressure of the air changed again. Lucifer pulled away from his prize and roared. His knees snapped forward, pushing through more human flesh so that his animal-like legs were more pronounced and formed. Ripping through the dead feet, his sharpened hooves twisted into the floor like he was preparing to charge. From either side of his head, long black horns spiraled up and forward. Isabel's tears were thicker now; salt water turning to blood, streaming from her eyes and into her hair which was matted against the stone beneath her.

Thunder ripped across the sky and she looked toward the Heavens. The clouds rolled in thick with lightning snaking through the darkness burning her eyes with its light. She felt ashamed and dirty, causing her to turn her eyes away from God's wrath. In the distance she could hear the banging against the door through the chaos. Marciel, Felipe, and Miriam had been trying to break in the entire time. She watched as the hinges reverberated with each bang. There was no more hope, Isabel thought. Her brother's devoured body lay just mere feet away from her and she was nearly dead on the stone behind the hideous beast that had molested and violated her.

A trumpet sounded from the skies and the Devil bellowed in response. His whip-like tail lashed around his ankles and the clergy gathered nearer to him, their robes flapping behind them until they were transformed into feathery black wings. Their metallic eyes burned with hatred for the sound that echoed through the air. Isabel could feel the presence of Heaven's army and its impending arrival in every pore of her crippled body. The Devil stood defiantly awaiting the battle that was to come. The ominous chanting continued from the dark angels that were once his clergy, their staves gnarling into weapons. Isabel felt her stomach twisting and churning until she grew ill. Rolling to her side, the spilled out a black liquid that looked like congealed blood and tasted like death on her tongue. She curled into a fetal position only to feel the swelling in her abdomen.

The door burst open and Marciel flew to the ground with the momentum of their final impact. Getting to his knees, his eyes grew wide at the sight of his brother; once the most beautiful angel in Heaven, his form now a mangled mass of flesh; half beast, half angel. Lucifer laughed at his brother's reaction. "Brother! Are you not happy to see me?" he growled.

Marciel went to his feet, his human heart fluttering in his chest. Fear gripped him from the depths of his soul and he no longer felt Heaven within. Gone were his wings, his armor, and his sword.

He swallowed hard and pushed his spine erect, facing the monster before him and prayed "Dear Father, grant us your mercy. By your will, defend me. By your might, defend my cause."

Lucifer howled in rage, "Will you slay me, Marciel?"

He snorted through flared nostrils, taking a few steps forward, his hooves grinding on the stone beneath his immense weight, before he leaned in close, “Poor, helpless, Marciel. No wings, no weapons! What shall you defeat me with?”

Marciel had little left for dignity at the humiliation of his brother and all that he had borne witness to. He turned toward the skies that screamed with the sound of wings. The angels of Heaven were coming. His eyes fell to Isabel and saw her lying there curled up with arms grasping her belly which had grown full and round. The full scope and magnitude of the severity of the situation finally dawned on him. She was pregnant!

“What have you done, Lucifer!” he screamed.

The Devil threw his head back and laughed, then rushed at Marciel like a bull. “Time for words is done. You will die with them, Marciel. And I shall reign over you in Hell!”

Marciel ran backwards, no weapon within his grasp. His back met with the wall roughly, and he turned his head, raising his arms to shield his face just as one of the Devil’s horns pierced through him, almost severing his spine. He could feel the blood trickle out from the wound, and his sight grew dim. Both hands grasped the horn and he tried with all his mortal strength to pull it free. The fear of dying in this human guise was near again, lingering over him like a pendulum.

Father Dulante rushed up from behind with the clergy of dark angels following him, snapping at his heels. The Hellhounds chased Miriam as she ran to Isabel's side. Father Dulante thrust the only weapon he had; a large candlestick, into the Devil's side. Lucifer barely felt the metal pierce his flank and twisted, throwing Father Dulante across the room with a large, clawed hand. The disfigured Harlot was already slithering hungrily toward him when the dust of the exploding floor temporarily blinded her. A hole was blown through the thick stone with a flurry of Heaven's angels flowing through it like a tornado. The wind from their wings blew debris everywhere.

The sound of the trumpet rang out again, the assault of wind and noise sending the dark angels reeling back for a moment. Brilliant wings rushed upward with spears and swords thrusting at the enemy. The Devil jerked his horn from Marciel's abdomen and the wall then rushed into battle against the army of his brothers, leaving Marciel to slide to the ground. Crawling through the rubble he would continue toward Isabel.

With the Hellhounds now engaged with Heaven's army, Miriam was already there trying to press her hand to open wounds. There was so much blood; she didn't know which one to attend to first.

One of the Devil's angels turned catching sight of Marciel and kicked him. The crunch of the broken ribs sent him breathlessly against the floor, recoiling in pain. Bleeding and gasping for breath, the flurry of white feathers filled his sight as one his brothers came to save him. The dark angel was pushed back with several attacks before the holy one swung out to the left, decapitating the enemy.

The beheaded body fell to the floor and black snakes slithered out, hissing and rearing back from the light. Marciel would not give up even though he was mortally wounded. He continued through the battle toward Isabel as three of his brothers now focused on Lucifer. They were being defeated when the fourth trumpet rang out. Through the windows, two larger angels crashed through, their wings nearly overcoming those already inside. The smaller angels fell back, focusing on the remaining dark angels and Hellhounds. A spark of hope flooded through Marciel giving him more will to go on; Gabriel and Michael were now taking point in front of their former brother.

Rushing toward Isabel, Marciel could see that her stomach was growing still. She looked like she was nearly full term!

"Dear God.." he said, wincing in pain while looking down at her. Isabel was barely conscious and Miriam was weeping as she helplessly held torn rags from her dress as bandages to the battered body of her friend. Blood pulsed from every wound making Isabel deathly pale. Looking at Miriam, he was clueless. What could he do now? Did he try to kill the creature that was being formed within her and risk killing Isabel as well? But she was already near death. Killing was a sin. Marciel's head fell back and he cried out, "WHY!?"

Curling his fingers inward and gritting his teeth, he ran to grab anything he could that would tear through the bulging flesh. The unborn must be destroyed! He stumbled as he ran, slipping on his own blood, every breath he took causing white flashes of pain from the broken ribs.

He saw Father Dulante's body on the ground and he ran toward him.

Scraping his knees as he fell to them, he shook the priest, "Wake up! Wake up, Marcos!!"

To Marciel's relief, Father Dulante's eyes fluttered open and with his friend's help, rose to his feet still clutching the candlestick. Marciel grabbed it from his hand and the two men ran back toward Isabel. The remaining Harlot had Miriam and was dragging her away from the unconscious woman. Father Dulante ran to help her but it was too late. His eyes met Miriam's just as the Harlot spun her head, snapping her neck. Miriam went limp suddenly and was dropped to the floor. Marcos made the sign of the cross and thrust his crucifix outward causing the Harlot to recoil and hiss violently.

Marciel was staring down at Isabel who was pushing through unconsciousness just as he was about to plunge the candlestick into her. Her eyes widened and she reached out toward him, "No Marciel! Please!"

He paused, struggling to push himself to do it. The inner struggle was too much and he cried out again, "It must die!" tears rolled down his cheeks, knowing what he must do.

"Please!" she pleaded with him.

"I ..I need my last rite, Marciel. I cannot die like this.." her words were coming in short bursts of breath.

Beside them, Father Dulante was still struggling against the Harlot. Her body crouched low and she was snapping at him, swiping with her nails to disarm him of his cross. Father Dulante's prayers were fervent and rushed, knowing she would gain more strength and come at him over and over until she could get a grasp on him.

Amidst the chaos, Marciel placed a hand on Isabel's head and recited the last rites between sobs, "Oh Lord Jesus Christ, most merciful, Lord of Earth, I ask that you receive this child into your arms."

Isabel's eyes began to close before they suddenly opened wide. Her body trembled wildly against the slab, something was slithering under the skin of her face. Marciel jumped back and cringed at the stab of pain causing him to cough, violently. Each contraction resulted in more agony. Isabel's torso flew up to a sitting position before flailing back to the stone, crunching the bone in the back of her skull. She lay still for a moment before repeating the action, arms extending out to grab him but he narrowly escaped. Her head thrashed side to side and white foam bubbled at her mouth with a gurgling noise.

Marciel reacted quickly seeing that demons had inhabited her, keeping their grip on the woman. If he didn't exorcise them now, they would drag her soul to Hell for eternity. Lost in a mortal shell, he didn't know if he had the power to do it but he had to try. Raising his hand to make the sign of the cross, Isabel let out an unearthly screech that rose above the battle surrounding them, "I cast you out, unclean spirit along with every Satanic power of the enemy, and all your fell companions; in the name of the Lord Jesus Christ!"

The incantation sent the demons into hysterics. Isabel's fingers curled and stiffened as if grasping for the sky. Her jaw opened unnaturally wide, unhinging from the joint of her jaw. The entirety of her eyes growing black, she wailed in torment.

Meanwhile, the Devil responded with a guttural roar, rushing against Michael and Gabriel with lowered horns. The archangels moved with little room to spare and sent their weapons into the thick meat of the Beast. Black ichor oozed from the gashes. Infuriated, the Devil threw his horns against Michael, puncturing his abdomen and lifting him off the ground before tossing him in the air.

Marciel's hair blew away from his face as he continued his attempt in extracting the demons from Isabel, "Be gone! And stay far away from this creature of God for it is HE that commands you!"

The Unborn within Isabel's womb stretched against the tissue that held it. Contractions began to push down on it, forcing the birth to begin. Father Dulante continued to hold the Harlot at bay, shouting his own incantations. He'd take steps toward Marciel and Isabel hoping to aid in the exorcism while fending off the possessed nun. The men were becoming overwhelmed and overpowered. Exchanging glances, they persevered, "Therefore, I adjure you, profligate dragon, in the name of the spotless lamb, who has trodden down the asp and the basilisk, and overcome the lion and the dragon, to depart from this woman.. to depart from the Church of God!"

Father Dulante made the sign of the cross and the Harlot shrieked. Arching her back, her spine cracked as the bones broke. The woman's body fell to the floor and she coiled like a snake, dragging her useless legs like behind her like a tail, her tongue split and forked, whipping about as she writhed. Slithering toward Father Dulante and Marciel, the priest let out a shout and ran toward her. Raising his hand, he lanced the Harlot's throat with the crucifix, "Tremble and flee as we call on the name of the Lord, before whom the denizens of Hell cower!"

He pushed the crucifix deeper and the creature hissed and undulated, spitting black, tar-like liquid at him. Father Dulante turned his face to avoid it.

"The word!...made flesh!...commands you!" he cried, dealing a final stab into the creature's throat until its body grew still and fell at his feet.

Panting, Father Dulante spun around to assist Marciel. Isabel's body was contorted, her legs falling wide, and her heels pressing into the stone. She groaned and growled through the birthing of the unnatural spawn that forced blood from her cervix in vile offering of the life it would spring forth. Lucifer fought desperately to get to Isabel and the monster that was emerging but the Archangels would not falter. Every rush he made to get past them was thwarted by the point of their swords. The Beast would stomp its hoof into the ground and pivot, trying another angle but they'd herd him back, again.

Exploding into full madness, the Archfiend chanted and the earth trembled. Fire caught to the curtains and then rolled out across the floor toward Michael, setting his wings aflame. A white light stretched out from the Angel's chest and fought to put out the fire while distracting him from Lucifer's next move. He coiled his tail around Gabriel's ankles and ensnared him, dragging him to the ground. Escaping the fight, he bore down on Marciel who fought to exorcise Isabel before it was too late.

Father Dulante tried to push the former angel out of the way. Looking into his friend's eyes, he saw the shock and sadness as a result of the attack. Still holding onto him, Father Dulante shook his head and felt the man sliding to the floor. He tried to hold him up but it was too late. Lucifer had impaled him with both horns, barely missing the priest when they found their way through Marciel's chest. Father Dulante fell to his knees over Marciel.

They failed. It was over.

A sudden cry followed a gasp for air as the Anti-Christ was born.

FATHER DULANTE: MILES AWAY

Father Dulante stood among the carnage. Everyone was gone. The crucifix in his hand swayed and trembled with his hands and he watched as the blood dripped off each bead. There was no more distinguishing whose blood it was; Angel, Demon, Human..it was all mingled and falling to the floor in a steady *pat, pat, pat*.

His ears could no longer stand it and he threw it to the ground. Turning his war-tattered body around, he took in the sight. Pure white wings, ripped from Angelic beings. Raven colored wings broken and disfigured. The Harlot was lying in a pool of coagulated red. He could feel his heart racing and the numbing pain trail out along his arm and throughout his chest. Mangled fingers clutched at himself but he knew what was happening. He was having a heart attack.

Fear struck him once again. There was no one there to issue *his* last rite. Desperately, he fell to the stone floor and slid his free hand through the sticky mess of death to find the discarded crucifix but the room was quickly growing dark.

"No.." he cried. Forcing his will forward to continue his search, he felt the sudden warmth of a hand. Gazing up, he saw one of the Angels. Slowly, it raised a finger to his lips, and then pulled Father Dulante into his embrace. The Angel spoke but all Father Dulante could hear was music.

They speak in music. He thought to himself before he gave in to the darkness.

Seven days later – or so he was told – Father Dulante awoke in the warmth of a bed he'd never known in his whole life. The sheets were made of the finest cloth and the comforter was a bright white, full of feather down. The smell of beeswax filled the air and he tried to focus his vision to see further out. Heavy red curtains made from chenille, shielded the windows from any light that might be beyond them.

"Wh-where am I?" he uttered.

A voice answered him and he flinched. He had not been aware that anyone else was there with him.

"Rome." Was the reply.

Confusion was evident on Marco's features until it became clear then that he was at the Lateran Palace. Once his vision began to return to more than the blur of the room beyond a few feet, he could see the face of the man that spoke to him.

LITTLE SOUL: IT BEGINS - ISABEL

There was the light again.

The pain coming from Isabel's lips was real. She could taste the dried blood. The ticking of a clock was somewhere off in the distance, like the heart of a hummingbird. Time was so relative, now. She had slipped in and out of consciousness so many times, there was no way to keep track.

Day. Night. Winter. Summer.

This is how time went for her. Fleeting like winter's snow falling timelessly to the earth below. Time drifted on seas and through gentle breezes. Wafting through branches like a dream before it was shredded by reality and pain. It was harder for her to fight for consciousness. Her battered body hurt so much that she nearly gave in a thousand times. The images that filled her mind were horrific. The voices spoke things that she could not erase from her thoughts; unspeakable things.

Prayers only brought her more pain and torment. Yet, here was the light again. Shuddering, she turned away from it and a voice called to her from the distance. Isabel looked down at her body and the blood was still there. Mangled fingers trembled when she took in a full inspection of herself. Dirt and blood were smeared along her limbs, her dress was tattered and filthy, and she was bruised wherever she could see exposed skin. Dazed and confused, she shook her head slowly, trying to force understanding upon herself but the pain was setting in. The ringing in her ears became louder until it was piercing her mind making her scream while bringing her palm up to her head. She was trying to shield her ear from the noise when the touch sparked with it a new pain causing her hand to jerk away. Bringing it back toward her face, she could see the blood and pus, sticking against her palm.

Her mouth opened and she prepared for a wail but nothing came out. Only the sound of winter surrounded her. Everything else was eerily still and without noise. The darkness began to depart slowly, pulling back to reveal the snow blanketing the earth all around her and enveloping the rest of the world in its icy embrace. She was lost.

Taking a step, her blackened, frost-bitten toes pushed into the packed snow leading her forward with extreme difficulty and pain. The sound of a child crying from somewhere slowly pushed past the ringing in her ears and she began to remember. The sound of the cry brought the images rushing back. She hurried toward the echoing sound lost in a panoramic field of white. There was no direction. She took a few steps forward and the cry would come from the other way but when she'd turn and run toward it, it would stop and come from someplace else.

The cry was growing weak. Desperation rose up inside of her and she pushed toward it as fast as she could, staining the virginal snow with fresh blood from her thighs and torn soles. From nowhere, tall iron gates appeared and beyond it a lone tree. None of it made sense but all reason left her when the child cried out again.

Tugging the gates open, she saw a shadow to her left followed by another. From her right, another shadow flickered past and she spun that way. Between them all was the tree with the babe flailing in agony. Her breath came faster as the panic started to build and then the shadows made themselves known. First, she saw the eyes; gold and crimson peering at her with predatory hunger. The muzzles were next and hung low beneath large, hackled necks.

Wolves.

Isabel paused, frozen as she assessed what her next move was. Each cry the child released caused the animals' maws to salivate more. Their lips curled upward in menacing "smiles" and she could see them hunching low, getting ready to attack the helpless infant. In an instant, Isabel sprung forward pressing against the prickling cold. The air burned her lungs and she raced the hounds in attempt to save the baby that was ripped from inside of her. She could see the snow around its small, convulsing body melted by the blood and fluid of its birth. Her eyes locked on his pale, round face and she tripped then let out a scream watching the wolves close the distance. Isabel pushed to her feet, once again. Winded and hysterical, she resisted the excruciating pain until she fell on top of her baby and cradled him in her arms.

The world stopped for just a second when her eyes met his; so blue like the sky looking into hers. She smiled, pulling his face against her breast and there was warmth followed by a small tickle before she realized he was suckling at her nipple. Isabel's eyes closed and she rocked him back and forth. The babe made soft cooing noises and nuzzled in further as it fed and its scent lifted up into her nose, filling her with the bond that only a mother and child could form. It was a bond that gave her the drive to protect him from everything, even at the cost of her own life.

Time remained frozen for that single moment; perfect and euphoric. Allowing her head to fall back, her eyes opened toward Heaven so slowly that she had no time to react to what was about to begin. The demonic faces were inches from hers, hanging from the branches of the tree like bats; they attacked as soon as her vision focused. Talons slashed at her flesh but she held tight to her baby, protecting him from harm with her own body.

"NO!" she screamed. But she knew that eventually they would get to him. She was already broken and battered at the hands of Hell and all of Lucifer's minions.

She felt a pain at her nipple like something being torn and she looked down. The baby's eyes rolled up inside his head and made the dark, blue-black circles look even more hideous. Teeth dug into her areola, tugging and pulling with an unholy suckle, gurgling on her blood. She screamed and tried to pry him from her breast but it was growling and clawing with his small nails for more. Wrestling the child – the "Thing" – free from her breast, she watched as the demons dove in for him. One grasped his arm and snatched him into the air with the others following. In shock, Isabel cried out with outstretched hands until she fell; face forward, into the snow again.

THE UNSAINTLY

THE UNBORN

THE ANTI-GOD

They're coming soon

This book is dedicated to:
my *beautiful* family, my *amazing* friends, and my *soulmate*
to my father, step-father, and grandmother who aren't here in the flesh to share this moment but **are** here. *I feel you*.

Without **Depeche Mode**, the hypnotic voices of **David Gahan**, **Martin Gore**, and the talent of composer **Christopher Young**, there would not have been a book at all. Their music inspired me, entranced me and kept my fingers possessed from the first page to the last.

Without Alan Daniels and his incredible imagery, this idea would've remained dormant within the dungeon of my mind. Thank you for being so gracious in allowing me to share your work, with the world when the second book makes its debut. I hope that it arouses all the emotions that it did for me.

Last but not least, for everyone that stood by me from day one, waiting for this book to be completed, who never gave up on me, and who laughed along with me even when the first edition came out hacked and mangled. You guys are true friends, fans, loved ones.

My *special* dedication shout outs:
My Bad Thing 2 – Mr. Paul McVay, the Lovely Heather McVay, Brandy Short, Brenda Campbell, Maureen Lanza, Justin Vasquez, Gypsy Jones, Kat Moore, Jason Barnard, Jesus Blancas

Thank you for not only contributing emotionally but in other ways as well. There are no words.

34405530R00150

Made in the USA
Charleston, SC
08 October 2014

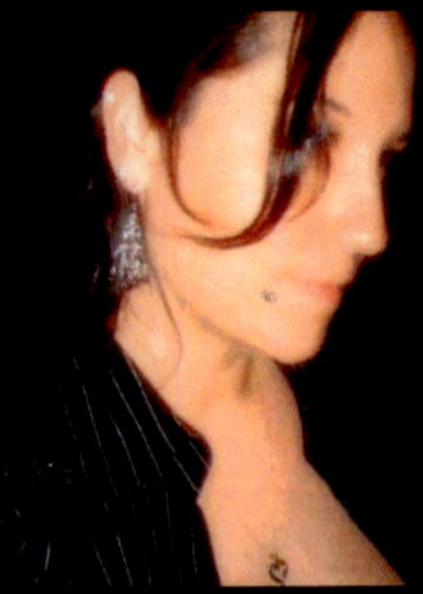

The Unsaintly is the journey of Isabel, the daughter of Louis VII and Blanche of Castile, who devoted her entire life to the servitude of God. When Isabel begins to suffer from stigmata, she learns that it is just the beginning of her role in the fight between Heaven and Hell. Her sacrifice is not great enough when the abuse inflicted by the stigmata she suffers leaves is then replaced by the real horrors inflicted by God's rival; Lucifer.

All that she's learned up to this point will be tested along with her faith, in this horrific story of good, evil, and everything in between.